All The King's Horses

and Other Stories

Winners of the 2005/6 Short Histories Prize

Edited by Clem Cairns

Assistant Editors
Lorraine Bacchus
Tessa Gibson

Fish Publishing
Durrus, Bantry, Co. Cork, Ireland
www.fishpublishing.com

Published in Ireland by
Fish Publishing, 2006
Durrus, Bantry, Co. Cork

Fish Publishing is assisted by The Arts Council of Ireland

ISBN 0-9542586-4-9

A catalogue record of this book is available from the British Library.

Cover design by Jula Walton

For details on Fish Publishing's literary competitions and editorial consultancy
see:
www.fishpublishing.com

Or write to:
Fish Publishing, Durrus, Bantry, Co. Cork, Ireland
info@fishpublishing.com

Contents

Foreword

Most writers can identify the pitfalls of historical fiction wonderfully well. They can give you a list of temptations that must be resisted; indeed, some give lectures and produce manuals on the subject. Then, blind to their own advice, they fall head-first into the pit themselves.

The problem is, it's not easy to write fiction set in bygone ages without doing all the things that good narrative sense tells us not to. Those who learn too much from the past are condemned to repeat it. That is, those who have carefully studied, eg, 17th century Flemish butchers as "background research" for their story are often condemned to tell us every little thing they've learned about butchery, the Flemings, and the 17th century in general. They may flatter themselves that this is precisely what they've avoided. They may assure us that what they show in the narrative is only the tip of the iceberg, and that the vast bulk of their research is actually submerged, unstated, implicit. They may speak disparagingly of those *other* historical writers who just can't help pointing out period details twenty times per page. But then you start reading, and before you know it, you are inundated with information that the characters themselves would never remark upon. Illiterate peasants mention, in the course of unlikely conversations, what year it is and which king is on the throne. Pampered ladies who, in real life, would have regarded their servants the way we regard the electrical cord behind the fridge, feel honour-bound to describe everything their maids are doing. Everyone seems bizarrely compelled to analyse every aspect of their daily lives: the composition of their clothing, the contents of their food, the manufacture of virtually every object they touch. And, of course, every sentence spoken by everyone is stuffed with archaisms. Even Babylonian slaves and Vikings orate like pompous Victorians.

When writers of historical fiction do this, it's not because they've gone mad. It's because they fear – quite reasonably – that if they don't keep reminding you of the past, you will get lazy and see the present. The present is our default setting. It is what we picture in the absence of specific information to the contrary. "A young man kissed his girlfriend in the street": we see a modern man, a modern girl, a modern street, even a modern manner of kissing. Ancientness needs to be added, and kept topped up.

What, then, is the secret of a good historical story – a story that keeps us securely inside a bygone world, while not annoying us with constant reminders of where we're supposed to be? How can an author recreate a past era in such a way that it isn't a theme park?

For answers, I invite you to turn to 'All The King's Horses', Jo Campbell's winning story in the Short Histories Prize. In transporting us to a famous late-medieval battle and keeping us there, it does as much as it needs to, never more, never less. The beginning of the first line, "We came over the downs at dusk on the third day", establishes a great deal in eleven simple words. The triple alliteration is reminiscent of Anglo-Saxon poetry, planting a subliminal suggestion of where we are in time. The use of "we" alerts us to the fact that this tale will convey the experience of more people than just an individual. The down-to-earth language (ten of the eleven words are monosyllables) signals that these are common folk. "On the third day" alludes to two previous days which we'll never know about, because life moves on and the narrator is disinclined to waste time reminiscing. As the sentence opens up to acknowledge "the straggling lines of men coming from all directions to join in one long column", we join the throng. We don't know what's going on and why we're here, but then, neither do many of the soldiers. We've missed the start of this story, but if we fall into step, we're expected to catch on.

Having established the tone and the pace, Campbell recognises the reader's urgent need to see and hear the scene. "Around us on every side were points of light where soldiers already had their fires, and below us in the valley the flares of the shipyards and bonfires on the quays. We could hear the ring of the shipwrights' hammers and the shouts of the sailors, and could see the masts, still bare, standing like saplings against the evening sky. Beyond the masts stretched a great darkness, with the evening star hanging above it. Now and then one or other of the fires would burn up for an instant, and by its light we could see the wrinkled surface of the water moving, moving." Though only four sentences, it is the longest description in the story, if we define description as sensory scene-setting that is separate from character and action. Yet there is nothing gratuitous about it. Each of its components works very hard and very economically. It's not just a vivid picture: we can divine quite a lot about what is going on. And it makes sense that our narrator would note all these things: he has never seen them before.

Then someone speaks. "Is that the sea?" asked young Wat; he had been longing to see it, but now he was almost too weary to look. I had been carrying him on my shoulders for the last few miles." Here, so near to the outset of her story, Campbell manoeuvres the crucial emotions and themes into place: the vulnerable boy, the narrator who cares for him, the pitiless harshness of the endeavour, the ominous sense that no amount of promised glory can justify the sacrifice. All this, we absorb without fully knowing that we've taken it in. The story has us. We already understand it instinctively, even though we've barely entered its action.

I could write an in-depth analysis of what follows, every paragraph of it, and thus compose an introduction longer than the story itself. But the important thing to note, and to admire, is Campbell's sound instincts for what needs saying and what should be left unsaid. Too often in historical fiction, characters seem aware of the momentousness of the events they're embroiled in. Real life is seldom like that. People cope as best they can, living from minute to minute, performing the small tasks they're given, trying to get along with whoever is closest. For many writers, in thrall to history books, the story of this battle is the story of King Henry V. But in Jo Campbell's account, the king is never given a name, and the narrator hears of his prowess only second-hand. The battle as we experience it is fought by ordinary men – credible individuals whose ongoing concerns are food, warmth, a comfortable place to sleep. The name of a nearby village – Agincourt – is mentioned only once, in passing. That casual mention has power precisely because no particular import is placed on it.

Like all good stories about war, 'All The King's Men' applies to all wars. Matter-of-fact references to bowmen and falchions remind us at judicious intervals of the medieval setting, but mainly we are enveloped in the perennial realities of soldiers killing and suffering as soldiers always do. This is an Iraq story as much as it is an Agincourt one. It is a passionate indictment of the damage that is done to men's bodies, minds and morals by war, but there is no polemical posturing in it. The narrator fights well, and does what he must. At the end, he displays what he has become with no self-pity. He can't change things now: his pain is History.

Not all of the stories in this anthology are quite as finely judged as 'All The King's Men'. A few display their research more than they need to. It's no crime; some of the most celebrated, and best-selling, historical novels ever written might have benefited from more restraint. But each of the pieces here has been chosen for its excellence. And they are a delightfully varied assortment, ranging from deadpan simplicity to Baroque complication, raw horror to sophisticated humour, slice of life to clever artifice. More than usual for an anthology, this is a compendium of all the different ways that fiction can succeed.

Take Imogen Robertson's 'The Monkey'. It could scarcely be more different from 'All The King's Horses' – except in its quality. Reading this wicked little tale of a dastardly Regency rake and his ill-fated purchase of a supernatural statuette, we never lose our awareness of being manipulated by an artificial construct, a neat device. Yet Robertson's relish in screwing the plot tighter and tighter against her protesting villain is obvious; 'The Monkey' is the equal of Roald Dahl's best revenge tales. And, crucially, Robertson takes care with her characterisation and her dialogue: the plot may be rigid as a steel trap, but there is nothing mechanical about the way these people behave and speak. This story has life. We suspend our disbelief for the sheer thrill of it and, more importantly, we care.

One of the mainstays of historical fiction is filling in the gaps of ill-documented lives of famous figures. Phil Jell slyly plays with this narrative tradition in his vividly evocative 'Altarpiece'. A boy, known only as M, works as a lowly apprentice in the studio of a Renaissance painter. To the mingled alarm and wonder of the master, this "naïve, gangling, simple" lad produces work of sublime beauty, far superior to those of his employer. Thus, a murky drama of encouragement and abuse begins. And, up until the thought-provoking climax, the reader cannot help speculating on the true identity of the young genius … Similar territory is explored by Clare Girvan in 'Titian's Rose', in which the painter recalls the infamous "Pietro Aretino, Tuscan, Venetian, writer, pornographer, poet, dramatist, womaniser, blackmailer and flatterer, libel-monger and man of letters, as unscrupulous as a stoat; my dearest friend." This tale of lust, love and cuckoldry is narrated in old age, when memories of lost companionship and the nearness of death grant Titian the ability to forgive long-ago betrayals. Forgiveness is often portrayed as an act of grace, but Girvan shows us that it can be a matter of weary pragmatism, a conservation of energy by a battered old soul.

Feminist scholars have pointed out that history is often "his" story. Men have traditionally used the Law, social structures and business practice to disempower women. Sheila MacAvoy and Janette Walkinshaw explore these infuriating inequalities in contexts hundreds of years apart. MacAvoy's 'In The Valley of the Trinity' takes us to the gold prospecting days of America's wild west, where prostitutes struggle to survive in a society which, for all its frontier newness, is already rigged against them. This patiently crafted piece has the feel of well-documented, reconstructed fact, enlivened by prose of laconic eccentricity: "He had black eyes and whiskers the same." Walkinshaw's 'Refugees' is set many centuries earlier, when the Lord of Galloway dissolves a Dumfries priory and then casts the nuns out into the harshness of the workaday world. Here, too – as always when women are rendered destitute – prostitution enters the picture, but Walkinshaw handles her characters' plight with tact and subtlety. Despite its medieval setting, this tale describes an ever-recurring journey; the nuns are refugees not just from the house of stone which they'd imagined "would stand forever", but also from their former value systems and ideas of selfhood. History, as seen by most of the writers in this anthology, is not the building up of a dream, but its dissolution; not a journey to an exotic clime, but a diaspora from a disintegrating homeland.

Two pieces with the same title, 'Russian Tea', reached the competition's final selection. Emma Darwin's story, 'Russian Tea', is a bittersweet, understated portrait of Russian émigrés sleepwalking through a new life in London after their enforced flight from post-Tsarist Russia. Mikhael, groom to the aristocracy, dreams of noble St. Petersburg horses and, upon waking, takes the Piccadilly tube to the street pitch where he sells pencils, shoe polish and dominoes. His fall from the ranks of the exploiters to the exploited is sketched insightfully but without judgement, and his melancholy encounter with a fellow lost soul has just the right frisson of sexual tension. The opening lines of Mary Woodward's 'Russian Tea' eloquently encapsulate the way memoir shades into fiction: "I remember the story. I think I remember the story." The narrator toys with the idea of phoning her elderly aunt. After all, "she was there. It may have been more than sixty years ago but she has a good memory. She just might have the one or two details which will make it live. But then I pull back. No. She could say it wasn't like that. Not the way you heard. It was this. It was so. And what she says might not help." What follows is a self-confessedly unreliable but wholly convincing recreation of a World War II encounter, in which the tea of the title symbolises human potentials not

v

often seen in this collection: generosity, honour, promises kept.

In tale after tale, the characters' nobler instincts are undermined by the cruelty of larger forces they're caught up in. And nowhere more so than in Hugo Kelly's chilling tale of the Soviet gulag, 'Vanishing Point', in which Comrade Lesin from the Cultural-Educational Institute is given the task of motivating malnourished prisoners to dig a canal from the Baltic to the White Seas. Hiding his compassion under a veneer of cold indifference, he manages to achieve results while saving lives. But this is a world where any moral stand is fatally risky, so it's entirely appropriate that Kelly's narrator keeps us in the dark, maintaining an emotionally blank tone that only makes the horror of the scenario more potent. Like Jo Campbell, Hugo Kelly trusts his reader's intelligence enough to let the story speak for itself, without trying to pump up the pathos.

All the tales I've discussed up till now, different as they are, are examples of conventional storytelling. Not so Judy Crozier's 'Dreamed A Dream', a hallucinogenic vision of Lord Franklin's expedition trapped in ice floes. Essentially plotless, as befits the marooned crew, it grips us solely with the poetry of its prose and the atmosphere of long-simmered madness. The lonely grandeur of frozen seas, and the unravelling morale of doomed sailors, have rarely inspired a meditation as sustained as Crozier's, a vision of glacial delirium, full of remarkable lines like: "Our names are written with the finest of nibs on a map drawn in ice-white and blue."

This is just one of the ways a story can succeed. This anthology offers ten. The past is here. Begin.

Michel Faber
2006

Acknowledgements

The three independent judges, Barbara Erskine, Michel Faber and Rose Doyle, deserve considerable thanks for judging this inaugural Short Histories Prize. I want to extend a special thanks to Michel Faber who took a lot of time and great care to write a discerning and insightful introduction to this anthology.

Before the stories got to the judges, they were read by a panel of dedicated editors. These were Clem Cairns, Lorraine Bacchus, Tessa Gibson, Lothar Luken, Eithne Ni Murchu, Helen Kelly-Jones, Carmel Winters, Katie Gould, Tina Pisco and Kath Watson. Thanks to all of them for their interested and expert contribution.

The idea for the Short Histories Prize belongs to Richard Lee of the Historical Novel Society of Britain. Between him and Jock Howson, marketing director of Fish, the elements were pulled together for the competition that resulted in this anthology.

Four hundred people entered, and I would like to thank all of them for doing so. The short list is at the back of the book, and any writers listed there are names to watch out for. While the overall number of entries was not high, the quality uniformly was.

Many of the stories were entered on-line, and credit is due to Phoebe Bright of Vivid Logic, and Trevor Williams of www.traintrain.biz for developing and maintaining the Fish web site to the point where the entire competition could be run on-line.

In the office it was Clem Cairns and Lorraine Bacchus who ran the show, assisted occasionally by Tessa Gibson.

The design and typesetting was done by Jula Walton, and credit is due to her for her artistic vision and attention to detail.

All The King's Horses

Jo Campbell

We came over the downs at dusk on the third day, straggling lines of men coming from all directions to join in one long column. Around us on every side were points of light where soldiers already had their fires, and below us in the valley the flares of the shipyards and bonfires on the quays. We could hear the ring of the shipwrights' hammers and the shouts of the sailors, and could see the masts, still bare, standing like saplings against the evening sky. Beyond the masts stretched a great darkness, with the evening star hanging above it. Now and then one or other of the fires would burn up for an instant, and by its light we could see the wrinkled surface of the water moving, moving.

"Is that the sea?" asked young Wat; he had been longing to see it, but now he was almost too weary to look. I had been carrying him on my shoulders for the last few miles. Of the nine of us from our manor only two or three were strong young fellows like myself. Most were older men, bachelors or widowers, such as could be spared; one was lame, one slow-witted. Alun the bowman was the only one of us who had seen service; although a Welshman himself, he had fought for the old King when the northmen and the Welsh rebelled. And Wat made up our number, a boy only nine years old, sent because he was an orphan with no-one to speak for him.

We found our mustering-point, amongst the Duke of Gloucester's men, and made a fire and cooked what we had. Wat fell asleep where he sat, and I covered him with my old coat.

"He is too young for this," I said.

"The army will be his family," said Alun. "A rough one, but better than none."

I lay down at Wat's side, as I had each night on our journey. It was a mild evening, there was warm weather coming. By the light of the dying fire

1

I could see Alun's grey head and lined face. He had no wife or child, and lived far from his own people. I wondered if the army had been family for him too, and if he was hoping now to find it again. But I was too tired to think of it for long.

We woke in the morning to find Southampton busy as a Michaelmas fair, the roads and tracks crammed with men and carts, nobles on horseback with their followings of armed men, ladies in covered litters, servants behind them with tents and accoutrements in ox-carts; a mass of people that shouted and swore itself into order. In the most sheltered places stood the silken tents and pavilions of the nobles, bright with banners and streamers; on the hillsides were the bivouacs of the common soldiers, and in amongst them booths for every kind of trade, sutlers and armourers, smiths, saddlers and leatherworkers; men selling fish, men selling cabbages. The camp was like a great town, and everything was to be had for money.

"Who are those women?" asked Wat.

I hesitated. Alun looked sideways at me, and waited to hear what I would say.

"Some wives follow their men," I said.

"They are dressed very gaily, for housewives" said Wat. "Look, that girl in the scarlet bodice is beckoning. She knows you, Ned."

I felt myself reddening, not knowing how to explain to this child what the women were.

"Why don't you speak to her, Ned? You're not very civil."

Alun was grinning, and I saw that I was being made a fool of. Wat knew very well what the girl wanted with me. He had had to live by his wits, and in his short life had seen more of the world than I.

Alun took his bow and went off to practise at the butts laid out along the river, but Wat and I had no pressing duties, and went wandering agape from one sight to another. At first I was delighted with the camp, which held more richness, more different sorts and ranks of men, than I had ever seen. But as the days went by, and Wat found other youngsters to run wild with, I soon had my fill of novelties. We had left home knowing only that the King was raising an army, though we guessed it was for France, and I thought, in Southampton I shall find out his purpose, and feel myself part of some great adventure. But though there was business and bustle, though men traded with one another, drank and quarrelled, practised at arms, all these things seemed to be done for their own sakes: the camp existed only to serve itself. As June turned to July the weather grew warmer and warmer, and my restlessness increased.

"I would be better off at home," I grumbled to Alun, "helping with the haymaking."

"You are not the only one to think so," said Alun, "this place is like a beehive without a queen. If the King does not come soon his army will melt away."

But these idle days at least gave Wat the chance to see what he had dreamed of. Some of his new friends were locally bred, and they took us along the river, past the quays, to the place where it joined the sea. We were dumbstruck at the sight of that great stretch of restless water, washing against the shore and reaching outwards to the sky, and never the same in colour or movement two days or two hours together, but always cold to the touch and salty to the taste. Twice in every day it rose to cover the shore, so that there was nowhere to walk dry-shod, and then it was sucked gradually away again, leaving the sand behind it clean and firm like a new-swept floor, studded with little gleaming shells and, at the margin, great heaps of greeny-black weed full of little pods that crackled when they dried.

"What makes it move?" demanded Wat. "Where do the waters go?"

The boys scoffed at our amazement, but not one of them had an answer.

"It is a marvel of Almighty God," I said, as our parson does when he doesn't know what else to say. But Wat was no longer listening: he and the others had run off shouting to splash in the little waves as they broke. I hung back at first, shy of joining in their play, but the temptation was too great, and I too ran and splashed like a child.

That evening as we ate our supper a band of men marched in and encamped near our bivouac. Around us in the darkness men were laughing and drinking, swearing and singing, but through the row I could hear the language the newcomers were speaking, very light and quick like the sound of a stream in spate. I saw Alun's head come up at it, as a

3

hound's does at the note of the horn.

"Are those your people?" I asked him, and he nodded.

"Go to them, then," I said.

He hesitated, and I realised he was unsure of his welcome.

"It's a long time," he said, "since I spoke Welsh."

We sat on for a while, listening. At last, Alun stood up.

"They are the King's men, as I was," he said, "I'll try my luck with them."

He slipped away, out of my sight, and a moment later I heard his voice, a little unsure, call out a greeting in Welsh. Voices answered him, fell quiet as he gave an account of himself, and then rang out in welcome. It felt strange, as if the man we knew had been changed in the darkness for another. I saw that from now on I should be more alone. Wat had his tribe of boys, but I am a quiet man, then as now, and do not readily make friends.

Soon afterwards we learned that the King was coming at last. In a moment, the idleness that had enfolded the camp disappeared like mist before the sun. Our sergeants suddenly forgot their easy-going ways, and drilled and chivvied us from dawn to dusk. Our lines were put in order, and weapons and equipment issued; the shipwrights and armourers redoubled their efforts, working long into the night, and the whole camp buzzed with expectation.

"Will he have a gold crown, Ned, and a silk robe, like Herod in the play?" asked Wat.

"Perhaps not the crown," I said, scarcely less excited than he, "but he will have splendid armour, and he will ride a magnificent charger, and there will be jewels on his coat."

But when we were all drawn up in ranks to receive him, I mistook him for a groom, and looked beyond him for the King. For he was shorter and more slender than I and not much older, riding a bob-tailed brown horse and dressed plainer and more soldierly than most of his nobles. And at first I was bitterly disappointed. But when he rode close by me I saw an open face, a firm mouth, and a sharp glance that met mine as frank and friendly as if I had been his brother. He stopped to speak to one and another, taking notice of their weapons and clothing, and asking about their lodging and food. He recognised some who had fought beside him in

4

the past, at Shrewsbury or some other battle, and greeted them as old comrades. Alun was one of these, and I saw how he reddened and glowed with pleasure at being so acknowledged, hardened old soldier as he was. All my discouragement fell away, and I longed only to do something that would bring me too to the King's notice.

With the new heart and purpose that the King's coming gave us, our preparations were soon complete, and the order came to load the ships. That was heavy labour, dragging carts up the steep gangways and stowing away weapons and stores under the direction of the sailors, working in the heat of the day and always urged to hurry, hurry. And when all was done, we still had to wait for wind and tide.

Last of all, when we were ready to set sail, the horses were loaded. One of the Duke's chargers was brought to the gangway, a great stallion with muscles rippling beneath a skin of silk, but skittish and fearful as a two-days foal. Halfway up he took fright at the hollow sound of the planks beneath his hooves, threw up his head and lowered his haunches, and began to back down again. The fellow hanging on to his reins fetched him a great clout over the head with his whip, at which the charger screamed aloud and reared, sliding on the slippery wood and about to pull himself and his groom into the sea.

Even then, without the lifetime's experience I have now, I knew that the secret with horses is stillness and patience. For they are finely made and easily alarmed, as some men are, but brave and long-suffering if they are gently treated. I was so angry at the hash this clod was making of it, and so sorry for the horse, that I forgot my timidity, and stepped forward and offered my help.

"What business is it of yours, churl?" cried the groom, but with the charger just then swinging round and aiming a great kick at his arse, he was glad enough to chuck me the reins and jump ashore.

I gentled the horse and spoke softly to him. He stood still, trembling all over, and as he grew quieter I backed him down off the planks on to dry land, and led him gently up and down. Then I laid my head against his and talked to him till the trembling ceased. And then I told them to lay straw mats on the planks, to deaden the hollowness of the sound. And in the end he followed me up as quietly as a babe, with his breath whiffling softly at my shoulder, and where he went, the other horses were content to follow.

This was a simple enough thing, but it so happened that the Duke himself saw it, and sent for me. I knelt on the quayside before my lord, a strong man in his middle years, with a rich mantle belted about him. He asked me my name, and how old I was. I told him I was nineteen, as well as I could reckon.

"Well, Ned Shaw," he says, "you have a knack with horses. You shall be one of my grooms, and stay with my charger. It is a nervous brute and needs good handling."

He said this last over his shoulder to a little, bow-legged man who was standing behind him, and looking at me pretty sourly.

"This is my housemaster," the Duke went on, pointing carelessly at him. "You will obey him in all things."

My first thought was to keep Wat with me.

"Sir," I said, "there is a boy from my village, he is small but very strong, and quick to learn – if he might work with me – "

"A shipload of brats if you like," said the Duke, "only take proper care of my charger – for I see," said he to the horsemaster, "the other varlet would have ruined him, and spoiled his courage."

And he chucked a couple of coins on the ground before me, and turned away. I saw how little he thought of me, and said to myself, *he is not like the King.*

I would not go to sea again for any money. We were jammed with the horses in the stifling hold, in the darkness and the stink of dung and spew. It filled me with terror to know I was shut in, with only the ship's frail boards for protection from the water, and to hear the din – the creaks and groans of the timbers, the shouts of the sailors and the slap and crack of the sails – without being able to see or understand the reasons for it. But I had little time to nurse my fears. Wat was sea-sick, and could do nothing, and the other grooms, resentful on their comrade's behalf, gave me but little and grudging help, while William the horsemaster drove me on with oaths and blows, calling me ploughboy and damned hobbledehoy.

I was sure he would dismiss me as soon as we touched land, but when at last, after four days of contrary winds, we led the horses stumbling ashore, he clapped me on the shoulder, and told me I had done well.

I looked at him in amazement. He would not meet my eyes.

"The fellow you displaced was my sister's son," he said. "But he was a bloody fool with horses, for all that."

The army made camp outside the port of Harfleur, a rough and meagre camp with none of the splendour of Southampton, and there it sat day after day, hoping that time and hunger would lead the townspeople to give us the victory. But they answered all our attacks with defiance, and with sorties of their own. In siege warfare there is little need for horses, except the rougher sort that draw the engines, and so we grooms took the chargers into the meadows, where they had good grazing and fresh water.

"We must keep these beasts in good heart," said William. "The nobles will ride in procession through the town when we take it."

"And if we fail to take it?" I asked.

"They'll gallop for the ships, what else? So win or lose, young Ned, learn how to arm and caparison a horse, and take care of its equipment. You are only a ploughboy still."

Sickness in the town made its way to our forces; a bloody flux, which left those it did not kill exhausted and unfit to fight. The latrines overflowed and the whole camp became very noisome. I was glad to stay away, and kept Wat beside me as much as I could, though he grew bored and saucy, and ran off whenever my back was turned to go marauding and pilfering with his mates.

We could watch what was going on from a grassy knoll overlooking the main gate of the town, but for a month there was little to see but the army festering outside the walls. But at last a stir went through the camp, our ordnance and field engines were brought up, and orders came to have the horses ready the next morning. We groomed and fed them before dawn, and cleaned their tackle and laid it ready. Wat did his part, but with first light he gave me the slip, and I knew he had gone down to the camp, to be closer to the fighting.

We grooms took turns to watch the assault from our hill. I saw our men rush forward, again and again, under cover of the arrows of Alun and his comrades, and fall back time and again before the answering storm of arrows and stones from the ramparts. I saw our ordnance breach the walls, and men struggle and die in the breach. I had never seen battle before, and thought I would be terrified and full of pity. But it all happened far away, shrouded in smoke and dust, the men indistinguishable from one another, and though I could hear the roar of our ordnance, and the shrieks of the wounded, it seemed no more dreadful to me than a child's game played out with sticks and toys. At last bugles sounded, the noise and fighting ceased, and heralds shouted to one another with a great deal of bluster and defiance. There was silence for a while, and then the city gates opened, and toy men came out and knelt before a toy soldier who must have been the King.

A boy came running towards me; it was Wat, filthy with smoke and blazing with excitement.

"Get the nags down to the gate," he shouted, "the town has yielded. Did you see it, Ned? Did you see the King?"

"When?" I said stupidly, "just now?"

"Just now? He has been fighting all day, on foot like a common soldier – you should have seen it, you should have been there – "

I thought so too. I felt bitter disappointment, and disgust with myself for having watched that desperate fight in safety, as if it had been a show at a fair.

"What a man he is!" Wat went on, suddenly bursting out laughing. "Do you know how he got them to yield at last?"

"How could I?" I said.

"He told the burghers he could not control his men, if they had to enter by force," he said. "They were afraid for their wives and daughters."

I did not know what he meant at first. When I understood, I was horrified.

"He could not have threatened that," I said. "You misunderstood."

We rested for a short time in Harfleur, nursing our sick and replenishing our supplies. Then the King left it garrisoned, and led the rest of us out again, marching towards Calais. The terrain we passed through was like our chalk hills at home, but wider and more open, with small scattered farms where the people closed their doors at the sight of us, or shouted a curse. We set out in good heart, but in the silence of those wolds laughter and singing died, and the army which had seemed so mighty in Southampton shrank to a puny thing, a straggle of sick and weary men following limp banners. Discipline grew slack, and men marched in any order, Alun sometimes with his countrymen, sometimes with Wat and me. By now it was October, and it grew colder, with high winds and heavy rain, which added to our misery. After a week rations failed, and we lived on what we could find; roots and stalks left from the harvest, nuts and berries from the woods. Hunger and sickness made us slow.

On the tenth day I missed Wat, and when he caught us up again he was hiding something under his shirt. He pulled the cloth aside a little to show us: it was a chicken he had stolen from a farm.

"For shame," I said, "to steal from those who have little. What if it were your family?"

"I have no kin, and I am hungry," said he, quick and angry. "Alun and I will eat it, since you are so holy."

We did not speak for the rest of the day. I was angry with them, yet dissatisfied with myself; I had spoken to Wat too sharply, and without thought.

That night Wat and Alun plucked and dressed the bird and spitted it over the fire. I walked away and busied myself with the horses, checking that each was securely tethered, but the smell of the roasting fowl followed me and made me groan with hunger. The bird was scrawny enough, but what fat it had dripped from it into the fire with little hisses and splutters; do what I would, I could not close my ears to those tiny sounds. At last I drifted back, and stood in the shadows at the edge of the firelight, watching them as they took the bird from the spit and began to divide it.

Alun saw me. He twisted off a leg, and held it out to me.

"Come on, St. Ned," he said, "eat your supper."

I took it, and sat down with them and ate. After that I never asked where our provisions came from.

A few days later we were brought to a halt unexpectedly, and stood for a while at a loss. Rumours of all kinds spread from man to man, but gradually we learned that the French army was encamped in front of us, near a village called Agincourt, cutting off our advance.

Our camp that night was very silent, and Wat and I spoke in whispers, though the enemy was the best part of a mile away.

"How far their lights are spread," he said. And indeed, the glow of their fires lit up the valley.

"Do you think the King will offer battle?" he asked.

"I think he must," I said, "we are trapped here."

We sat silent, gazing at that spread of light.

"Your place is with the horses, Ned," said Wat. "No-one will blame you if you do not fight."

"I know," I said, but I thought, *I will blame myself.*

"There is no-one but you who cares for me," he said.

In the firelight his eyes were enormous, dark and shadowed. Marching and privations had hollowed his cheeks and temples, and he looked older than his years.

"I'll come back safe, I promise," I said

Very early next morning we made the horses ready and led them outside the tents of the nobles. Bugles were sounding in the French camp and as dawn broke we could see it stirring with activity like an ants' nest in July. Our hearts were down, and the nobles when they came armed from their tents looked little better.

And then the King came out, plainly dressed as was his custom. He looked about him with relish, rubbing his hands together in the chill morning air, as cheerful as if he were setting out for a pleasant day's hunting. He clasped his friends by the arm or shoulder and spoke gaily to them, telling them that few as we were, we would surely have the victory, and that all those who fought beside him would be as his brothers. He glanced around as he spoke, including the humblest of us in that saying. All our hearts were warmed by it, and it was repeated from mouth to mouth throughout the army, all that long morning.

Alun jeered.

"I suppose tomorrow you will turn up at the King's table, saying *I'm your brother Ned Shaw, come to supper,"* he said.

"I am not such a fool," I said, "he didn't mean that sort of brotherhood."

"Believe me, that is the only kind worth having," he said.

"Shouldn't you go to your place?" I said. I was angry with him, for I didn't want Wat discouraged and fearful.

"Plenty of time," said he.

We were standing with the spare horses on a convenient slope a little to one side of our battle lines. The French army was already drawn up at the far end of the narrow valley, the floor of which had been ploughed. The difference between our forces was plain. The French troops were packed close, elbow to elbow, with ranks of horsemen on the slopes to either side, while our lines were sparse and had great gaps in them. When the French saw how pitiful we were they put up a great shout of derision, and some of their gentlemen paraded on their horses in front of their lines very tauntingly. Despite what Alun said, it seemed to me that they might attack at any moment, and I sent Wat off in haste to join the other boys at the rear, where the baggage and stores were kept.

But Alun was right. The two armies stood in the growing light staring toward one another across the furrows, and no signal to engage was given on either side. A long time passed.

"Why do they not come on?" I asked. I had to lick my lips before I could speak.

"Too dainty to cross the mire, perhaps," said Alun.

I did not ask him, *why doesn't our King give battle?* because I knew the answer already. Looking at the French array, my mouth dry and an emptiness at the pit of my stomach, I knew that the King's brave face was a mask he wore to hide his fears, and that now the testing time had come, he hesitated. And I felt a sort of loving pity for him, alone with his burdens, and remembering the shame I felt outside Harfleur, I knew that I could not be a bystander again. So I took my leave, quietly, of each of the horses, and when Alun went to join the ranks I went with him, and took my place in the rear line of foot soldiers, with the bowmen behind us.

And the two armies stood till the sun was high in the sky, shouting defiance but making no move towards one another, and we were growing faint and sick with standing. At last the King came riding along the front line, as he had done at Southampton, stopping in the same way to speak to one or another. And then he turned to face the French, and raised his hand. The bugles sounded, we gave one ragged cheer for King Harry, and began to go forward.

I had imagined running forward, full of eagerness and ferocity. But our progress was terribly slow. The ploughed land was soggy, and gave under our feet. Ahead I could see only the backs of my comrades, bent with the effort of walking; on all sides I heard oaths and laboured breath, and the squelch and suck of our feet as we dragged them through the clinging mud. As we floundered closer to the enemy these sounds were drowned out by their pipes and drums, their triumphant singing and jeering. It seemed to me, peering ahead between my labouring comrades, that the whole mass of the French army was springing forward to meet us, like a hound unleashed at a deer, and I stood still, bracing for the shock as that great force swept over us and crushed us into the ground. But no shock came. They had left themselves no room on the narrow valley floor to come forward or draw their weapons; they were so many that they impeded one another, and struggled together in the mire. As they did so their horsemen, impatient, swept down from either side and the whole mass of men and horses met and mingled, foot soldiers overridden and riders unhorsed and helpless. And then from behind us came the twang, twang of the longbows and a flight of arrows went over our heads, dense as a flock of starlings, and for every arrow, it seemed, a man or a horse fell. And again and again as they struggled there came another murderous flight, laying them down in rows like corn before the scythe.

Seeing this we took heart, and plodded on with fresh will, climbing over the piles of dead and dying to fall on any that were still standing. These French soldiers fought bravely, but they did so as a man might fight for his life with brigands on a dark night, each for himself alone. The huge army which had struck such fear in us had lost all will and purpose; we were chasing a flying foe. And so ended a strange battle, in which all was owed to chance, and nothing to valour.

Our troops divided when we reached the village, some to continue the pursuit, some to return to our own camp, some to carouse on looted stores. I felt a savage thirst, but no hunger; I stayed only for a mug of ale, for I was anxious to find Wat and let him see that I was safe. Bone-weary, as if I was trudging home after a long day's ploughing, I made my way across the low hills that bordered the valley, keeping away from the battlefield as much as I could. I felt as if my heart was broken, and *if this is victory,* I thought, *what can defeat be like?*

The air was full of dust and the stink of blood. Men lay in the folds of the hills where they had crawled, cold in death or groaning and beseeching me to put them out of their pain. That I could not do, but I was more merciful to the horses, using my knife to kill some that were grievously wounded. They lay like cattle after the Michaelmas slaughter, mere hollow-eyed lumps of carrion, robbed forever of their beauty and swiftness. Others roamed riderless, lame or bleeding, with foam at their mouths, or grazed the slopes indifferently, broken reins trailing beneath their feet. All shied away at my approach.

With some trouble I caught one of them, and pulled myself achingly onto his back. Clumsy rider though I was, he seemed reassured by my weight in the saddle, and glad to be directed. And for me there was comfort in his warmth, his familiar smell, the closeness between us.

I pushed him on, expecting at any moment to be met by shouting boys, demanding to hear the great deeds we had done. I wondered what I could find to tell them, for to speak truly of what I had seen would have made me weep. But no-one came running towards me, and when I came to the place where the baggage was kept there was no sound at all. And as I came closer I saw cups and dishes, provisions and coverings scattered about, and there was blood between them on the grass.

I found Wat lying across a bundle that had been slashed open with a sword. He looked unharmed, as if he were sleeping there, but when I lifted him he was cold, and I found that he had been slashed open too; his guts were mingled with the fripperies he had died defending. I sat on the cold earth, with his cold body in my arms, and remembered how often he had lain beside me breathing and warm. I thought of his wicked ways and loving heart, and all my pains to keep him out of danger, and the long journey he had made to meet this death.

I cannot tell how long I sat thus. Someone must have gone to tell the King, for he rode by with his train while I was still holding Wat's poor body. I saw the light of victory fade in his face as he looked at us; he looked pale, and old, and careworn.

"Kill all the prisoners," he said, and my heart cried *Yes.* One of the

nobles cried out "My liege – " but the King held up his hand to silence him, and said again, very quietly, *"Kill all the prisoners."* Then he rode away.

I laid Wat's body out of harm's way till there should be time to bury him, and remounted my horse to go about that business. On my way I overtook some of the bowmen, going on the same errand. The prisoners greeted us with cheerful faces, for so far they had been treated courteously and in accordance with the rules of war, and their guards tried to prevent us, for they had great hopes of ransom. But the bowmen cried out *By the King's orders,* and went among the prisoners with their swords, and I and others joined in with knives and axes, chopping them down where they stood. They had all been disarmed, and could do nothing to help themselves, though they tried, hanging on to our arms or lunging at our throats, trampling the dead and dying in their efforts to get away, clutching at our hands or knees and screaming for pity, pity. It is the same word in their language as in ours, and it was that at last reminded me, *these too are men.* With the thought I faltered, my arm fell to my side, and a poor devil who had kept a dagger hidden slashed at me, slitting my arm from elbow to wrist. He was cut down before me instantly, and through the faintness and terror that befell me at the sight of my own blood, I heard Alun's voice and felt his arm on my shoulders.

He pulled me aside out of that shambles, and made me sit on the ground while he tore a strip from his shirt and bound up my arm, cursing under his breath.

"Why did you meddle in this?" he said, "This was work for me and my mates, not for a raw boy like you."

His falchion lay between us on the ground, the blade still bright with blood.

"It is the children," I said, hardly knowing what I said. "The children are all dead, and Wat is dead. The King sent us because of the children."

He laughed in my face.

"Do you think the King cares tuppence for Wat, or the others?" he said.

"We have killed the best of their fighting men. They will fight us no more, and the King's name will be terrible in France."

"No," I said. "I saw his face, when we found the boys."

"They were many, and we are few," he said. "The more we kill of them, the fewer of us will die. Believe it was done for our sake, if you like."

I looked at the heaped dead, where the bowmen were stripping the bodies, and I turned aside and puked on the ground.

"Lord," said Alun, "what a tender youth you are, still."

"This was a wicked day's work," I said, "the King did evil to order it."

"Ah, Ned," said Alun. "Do as I do; I loose my bow when I am told, and draw my sword when I am told, and sleep easy at night."

He sighed, and wiped his falchion on the grass.

"We are done here," he said. "Let's go and give Wat decent burial, before the crows find him."

I was young, my arm healed cleanly. That was the only scar I got upon St. Crispin's Day; judge whether I am proud to show it.

Vanishing Point

Hugo Kelly

The light hung in the air as if a canopy was suspended from the guard towers at either corner of the camp. As we walked, dogs barked angrily in the night. Gurov, the camp commander, waved his hand, interrupting the swarms of mosquitoes that rose like pale shadows before us. He was a small man with a wide-eyed stare not unlike the front lights of a car.

"So the NKVD thinks that this is the way to save the canal?" he said.

I fought a deep sense of fatigue. The journey from Moscow had been tedious and tiring and I was still feeling the effects. Trying to make common cause with Gurov was also proving difficult.

"Well there is concern that we can't build it within the time frame," I said and shrugged my shoulders in the uncomprehending manner of lower officials everywhere.

"General Andrei has been leading some new thinking on prisoners," I added.

Gurov scratched his two-day-old stubble and looked blearily at me.

"So Magadan camp is to become an experiment."

"I am to send a report to the General on how these new methods work," I said.

"That may prove to be a very short report" he said, and for the first time offered a reluctant smile.

Two guards straightened as we passed through the guardhouse, one dropping a cigarette into the mud. Within the compound the soft ground was rutted, curdled to a sticky mass. A rat scurried across our path. I saw that there was an old stone building standing in the compound.

"What's that?" I asked.

"What's left of the old monastery," he said dismissively. "We use it mainly as punishment cells. Every morning the prisoners gather for roll call

17

in front of it ... that was my own form of experiment," he said sarcastically.

Further on I could see other buildings that I guessed were the bathhouse and the kitchen. A prisoner pissing outside one of the huts glanced towards us and ran into the hut leaving a black stream on his ragged trousers.

Gurov startled me by roaring after him. "Use the latrines! You stink the place out. It's enough of a cess pool already."

Shaking his head he led me to the first barracks. I could see blurred faces peering through the narrow condensation-covered glass. Gurov grabbed the handle of the door and pulled it open. Immediately I was bitten by an acidic smell, a sour mixture of sweat and decaying sickness. A narrow corridor stretched down to the back wall. On both sides wooden bunks were stacked towards the ceiling. Heads lolled down at us from their perches, the yellow light weeping down on their drawn features. For a moment there was no reaction and then in a strange tired shuffle, they stumbled to the ground, a symphony of jerking limbs coming to a halt in front of us.

Gurov stood at the top of the room. He seemed suddenly depressed as if he had just realised that everyone here spoke a different language and that there was no point in saying anything at all. Head bowed, he murmured, "Comrade Lesin has been sent to us from the Cultural-Educational Institute."

His stumpy fingers waved me forward.

Calmly I walked through the assembled men, forcing each one to make eye contact. It was like moving through a patch of decaying trees that limply stood to attention. I could see no skin, only a layer of grime, lice-covered clothes, brittle arms hanging like branches from emaciated bodies. I stopped at the back wall and composed myself.

"You are the lucky ones," I said, "serving this glorious project."

I paused. No one laughed and I knew then that there were prospects here.

I told them that their previous errors were not worthy of thought. They must lose themselves within the glorious present. The canal would link for the first time the Baltic Sea to the White Sea; the entire project would link them to the heart of the motherland. They were carving out our very future with their picks and shovels and wheelbarrows.

And then suddenly there was a loud groan from the ranks of the prisoners. I stopped distracted, as a body clunked to the ground. Gurov let out a frustrated bellow. A prisoner had collapsed and was lying in a foetal position on the ground. There was a trickle of diarrhoea on the floor.

"Pick him up," Gurov roared.

For a few seconds no one was willing to help. Gurov shouted at a couple of men who resentfully bent down and lifted the prisoner onto a bunk. He raised his arms and they fluttered above him briefly before falling again. Gurov gave a sigh and looked at me.

"This is what I have to work with. An artist turned labourer."

"What is your name?" I asked.

The man's eyes were so bloodshot that they appeared almost black. There was no depth to his body and he lay on the wooden surface like a sheet of paper.

"Lukin," he whispered.

"So you are an artist?"

I detected a faint nod.

"Do you admire the work of Shiskin?"

He blinked in a confused manner and I wondered had he heard me at all.

"Such work suffers from Bourgeois images of the countryside," he said in a thin, whistling voice.

"Yes," I said, "I suppose you're right."

Gurov had lost patience and walked away. I was about to do likewise when Lukin's reed-like hand touched my wrist. He was flapping at his clothes with his other hand and he pulled out a small object, which I first thought was a pencil. He held it up to me and I saw that it was a paintbrush, one perhaps that a child would use.

"A gift for … an appreciator of art," he said.

I smiled in response, knowing it was a sort of plea, a cry from one intelligent man to another for assistance. We are the same it said. Help me and help yourself. But I had no time for such games. I shook my head, not granting him eye contact or any acknowledgement of his appeal, and moved on.

Outside it was a relief to again breathe fresh air. Gurov seemed more relaxed and he leaned into me. I received a fug of bad breath.

"You have a good turn of phrase," he said in a secretive voice, "but it is important that we begin to see results. The Urki are just animals. But at least they're stronger."

We walked on in silence and I waited a few tactful seconds before speaking.

"I do have some activities that might motivate the men."

Gurov raised a hand in acknowledgement then stopped and looked gloomily into the grey light.

"It is your experiment," he said and walked off without saying anything more.

My initial work was observation. I watched the four a.m. roll calls and how the brigades formed for the trek to the canal site. What I saw there depressed me. Men pulled at the clogged ground with rough hoes and spades, some using handmade implements. Mud-banks held by flimsy wooden uprights, teetered dangerously. Wheelbarrows overturned, men looked frightened. It was a form of chaos, just as we had heard in Moscow.

That night I wrote to General Andrei.

"We are using the same technology that the Egyptians used to build the pyramids. We must be radical if we are to build the canal on time."

After one week the reply came back. It was unusually short and terse, a few lines declaring how important the completion of the canal was. I studied its bareness, felt the anxiety of the crisp bureaucratic phrases. "Proceed under your own initiative" was the final line.

The next day I went to Gurov. He was in his office sitting behind his overcrowded desk. The room was stuffy. There were a couple of photographs, perhaps of family members which he did not comment on even though he saw me glancing at them. He seemed ill at ease as if the desk and chair were the wrong size and he could not get comfortable.

"Well," he said, "you have proposals."

"I have a new plan for the supply of food to the prisoners. I think it will improve work levels and reduce the level of sickness."

He smirked, emitting with little effort the weary air of a man who had heard it all before. Then I began to elaborate on my plans and his face

20

began to contract little by little. By the time I had finished it had tightened to a constipated grimace. His nicotine-coloured fingers tapped suspiciously on the desk.

"Are these really cultural matters?" he asked.

"General Andrei has granted me a level of discretion in such areas."

He sat upright and stared at me. "Apparently he has," he acknowledged and fell into an empty silence.

"I wish also to refurbish the bathhouse and kitchens."

He laughed at the obvious naivety of my comment.

"But I have tried. We are on a waiting list. Damn engineers. What can we do?"

"I believe I can put Magadan at the top of the list. Priority action."

"Oh," he said softly. He smiled broadly showing his surprisingly white teeth. "Well then there is little else to say."

"Thank you Captain," I said.

"No. Thank you," he replied, this time without smiling.

I introduced the food programme after meeting the leaders of the work brigades. Instead of giving each man food based on what he worked, we would give a subsistence amount and then, depending on productivity, provide a bonus to the individual work teams. The brigade leaders were responsible for work but also for keeping their men alive. As a final inducement, extra rations for the most hard-working brigade in a given week would be awarded.

"A little bit of capitalism," Gurov sourly commented, but said nothing else. It was hard to complain: the engineers had arrived even earlier than I had hoped and began work. This cheered everyone, even Buganov, the head guard. He was a Georgian with a quiet, determined face that would splinter into an easy laugh or grim anger depending upon the circumstance. I bribed him with vodka for his assistance and one evening, while both of us were tipsy, he mentioned that one of the prisoners, Ivana, was a medical student. I saw possibilities immediately. Within couple of days we had an infirmary started for the prisoners. There were few medicines and bandages, but at least bones could be set correctly and some symptoms of pellagra and scurvy eased.

Reports soon began to filter back that the Magadan camp was

outperforming all others. Only two men died that month. It was then, as my confidence grew, that an idea occurred to me: we had need of an artist.

That evening I called for Lukin to be brought to me. He shuffled into my room. He stood, half bent, his arms falling in front of him. Though I was six feet away I could smell him. "Have you not had a bath?" I asked.

He shook his head. His brigade was still denying him that. They were tired of carrying him, even under the new conditions.

"All right," I said, dismissing the issue, "You must paint a mural on the monastery wall. Something inspiring that the men can look at every morning, to prepare them for the day ahead."

His head tilted as if he had difficulty hearing me. Then for a moment he digested my words.

"I won't have to work then."

"Yes," I said.

"And food?"

"Your rations as always will be commensurate with your work. But I will see that you get enough."

This too he took a few seconds to ponder.

"The wall will need to be plastered and painted," he said in a bolder voice.

"Technicalities," I said.

"When do I begin?"

I shrugged my shoulders. "Why not tomorrow? Start on some initial sketches."

"Yes," he murmured, "I will start tomorrow."

The process was a test of patience. There was a paper shortage and he had to make do with the backs of old files I managed to locate. He was so ill that at first I doubted whether he was an artist at all. Gradually, as his strength improved, his hand lost the painful shake, and the forms became purer, more pronounced. At first eager workers framed the central painting which I presumed would be of the canal or some similar project. But then each day these figures became smaller and smaller until eventually they disappeared. The outline of the central image too continually changed. Perhaps he was waiting for me to reprimand him but I never did: I was simply too fascinated.

"You painted once?" he asked me perceptively.

"Once. Many years ago," I replied.

"And you stopped?"

"Figuratively I wasn't bad but perspective was my undoing," I said.

He gripped his paper and pencil trying to keep his shrunken hand steady. Delicately he drew axis lines across the page. He sketched a point pulling lines towards it. Even on the blank page I became aware of different dimensions, the extreme skill of his hand. When he spoke he seemed excited, as if thrilled by the chance of being listened to after so many years.

"This is your line of perspective, and then you locate your vanishing point where everything moves to."

I nodded. "I remember I found it hard to put into practice. Perhaps I never fully understood it."

"Perhaps if you try again" he whispered, "you will find that you can do it."

"Yes," I replied, "perhaps."

He smiled, showing a pair of black gums.

The next day I took the afternoon off and explored the higher ground that overlooked Lake Vygozero, a short distance away from the camp. I followed the winding tracks through the thin woods to the highest point of the ridge where activity of the canal seemed to blink in the distance. The scene was beautiful, forests mottling the white slopes, the icy imprint of the lake, the landscape uncurling like waves towards the horizon. The unlikely beauty of Karelia was becoming apparent to me. I was reminded of my younger years when I would go to the Academy in Leningrad and see the landscape paintings of Savrasov and Levitan. I thought then of the duty of optimism; of how we must make the best of life and duty. I would soon finish my report, and imagined with pride Andrei reading it, knowing that we had been right.

I made my way back to the camp in high spirits. Buganov was waiting at the gate. He began to walk towards me.

"Gurov wants to see you now," he said loudly.

I sensed a tension that made me uneasy.

"I'll see him in a few minutes," I replied.

"Gurov wants to see you now," he repeated.

This time there was a faint odour of bleach when I entered Gurov's office. He sat at his desk and smiled coolly. His manner was brisk, business-like and immediately I was on my guard.

"Have you sent your report back to Andrei yet?" he asked.

I shook my head. "I haven't finished."

"Ah," he said, "that is good."

There was silence. He pushed back his chair and crossed his legs.

"This may come as a shock but it seems that some of the leadership at the NKVD has been found to be engaged in counter-revolutionary activities," he said. "The Cultural Institute in particular has apparently been infiltrated at the highest level."

I felt a vibration of something within my gut. It was fear.

"Andrei and his elite have been … removed," he continued. "Their ideas – particularly their radical ideas – have been shown to be to the detriment of the Soviet Union."

I still did not speak, staring at his lean shoulders. He almost had the frame of a dancer I thought.

"If I were you I'd tear up the report or perhaps change it in light of the new circumstances."

"What … circumstances?" I asked.

He picked up a few sheets of paper, all the time looking at me with paternal concern.

"These are the new orders. The men are to work fourteen-hour shifts. The canal must be finished. It has been decided to lessen the depth by one metre."

It took me a moment to realise what this meant.

"But no reasonably sized ship will be able to sail on it … "

He frowned and I stopped speaking.

"The canal must be finished," he repeated.

"Yes," I said, "I understand."

"I have requested an extra two hundred workers. We will need room. Some of the men are very weak or sick. Perhaps they could be moved to another, more appropriate location."

I studied his face and he studied mine. Nothing was said for a few seconds. He leaned forward and picked up a pen.

"Perhaps then it would be good if I could say in my report that you supervised the operation and ensured that work levels were increased."

Through the window I saw that the brigades were returning. They were queuing at the bathhouse, then they would queue for food and Ivanov would make a medical inspection. In the midst of this activity Lukin would be putting the final touches to his mural. I could see it in my mind. The images of the workers had dissolved into the luscious yellow of cornfields. A twisting road bisected the scene travelling elegantly into the future. Then there were the children. At first you could not see them but if you looked closely you could see a boy and a girl holding hands, running along the crest of the road; running into the future. Above them was the perfection of a blue sky holding everything within its glow.

I fixed my eyes on Gurov's face and straightened to my full height. The vein in my temple tapped a faint, insipid headache.

"I am anxious to do my duty," I said.

Gurov smiled and reached for a file.

That night Buganov led the guards through the barracks, pulling out the most unfit workers. Most were dizzy from sleep and followed our instructions like children. We loaded them onto trucks and drove through the silence to the thin woods a few kilometres away. The forest greeted us with dour, unwelcoming shadows. The moon shone across the ridged snow, making it shine like silver. At a dip in the land we stopped and the men were unloaded.

The guards I could see were agitated. The months of boredom had been broken and they were energetically responding. The prisoners slipped pathetically in the deep snow, sinking knee deep within its grasp. Some were unable to free themselves and the guards, cursing as they did so, pulled them out by their necks and pushed them forward. The men faded into the darkness, becoming smudges within the night. A few wandered in odd circles, arms outstretched and I realised that the prolonged hunger had damaged their eyesight and that they could no longer see in the dark. I waited for protests, for begging, for tears but there was nothing only the soft farting sounds made by the crunching of snow underneath their feet.

I saw Lukin struggling in the snow. He seemed so thin and harmless in the darkness that no one noticed him. He looked at me and at first I thought he wanted help but then I realised he was holding something in his hand. His voice was shaky and I turned away in case I would hear him.

"Just get this over with," I said to Buganov.

The guards checked their guns, standing in a disorganised line. Laconically they began to fire at will. The echoes spun around the trees, eventually getting lost in the pit of darkness overhead. On and on the noise went until I was startled to find Buganov suddenly at my side. He looked content. Everything was quiet again.

"Better make sure they're all dead," I said.

The guards wandered through the bodies, finishing off the wounded. I walked after them and found Lukin still lying half-buried in the snow. Blood dripped onto the white surface, reminding me of spilt paint. I saw that in his hand he was holding the thin brush that he had offered me once before.

*

At the camp, I intended to go straight to my room. Instead I found myself at Lukin's mural. The yellow corn gleamed in the moonlight and there seemed a sense of magic about the dim image, hidden as it was by the darkness. I traced my hand along the road, finding the paint still sticky.

Behind me I heard Buganov leading the men back to the barracks. They were talking and joking among themselves, full of good humour now that the tension of the night was over. I knew they were looking forward to drinking vodka and singing sentimental songs, about home and girlfriends and how much they loved their mothers.

I stepped out in front of them.

"One more job," I said. "Someone paint over this immediately."

Buganov looked at me sulkily but didn't protest. I left them grumbling and walked back to my room. I found a bin and went outside. In a quiet corner I burned all my papers and letters, anything that could be used. Last of all I burned my unfinished report.

In the morning, the monastery wall was white, crudely covered in thick paint. Everything was as it once had been. I met Gurov and he nodded curtly not stopping to speak. My services, I knew, were no longer of any value. I walked on, out through the gates of the camp until I had travelled a couple of kilometres down the squalid, damp road. At some point I allowed myself to be diverted along a lesser route, no more than a rough path. There was nothing around me but boggy land, slight humped hills, covered in dirty snow. But when I listened I could hear the noise and activity of labour. For a few seconds I did not know what it was but then I guessed somewhere out of sight, in the distance the canal was being constructed. The utterances were fragile, almost sad in that empty place. It would take many lives but it would be ready within two years, useless as it would be. I stood there until flakes of snow began to wind down from the bruised sky. Then I turned and walked back to the camp.

There was nowhere else for me to go.

Altarpiece

Phil Jell

1

Jesu! How can the Saints even, arrayed in all their glory, intercede for the lowliest of the low? I am worse than a mad wretch. Can you still bear to listen to me? You, the patron intercessor of my profession, you must know, with all your compassionate understanding, the vicissitudes of this occupation of ours.

I am beginning this altarpiece – a privilege, a mark of great esteem the Confraternity bestows on me, truly a humbling commission – and as I stand here supposedly commencing work on the predella, my head is filled with nothing but jealousy and hatred.

It is the boy. Again. How despicable I am! My prayers fail me for weeks and then all I can do is bemoan my fate to have been saddled with this bloody child. Mother of God, but I'm a blasphemer, to speak so, even in prayer. You know me; I can only really pray when I paint, and I think you would be the most forgiving of me for it, though I doubt you are pleased to hear nothing but complaints and swearing. Yet what else can I do? It is the boy. I am tearing the hair from my head.

Vanity, it has been said, is Lucifer's favourite snare, and it is one that seems devised for those who live by their art. Had I more than my share? Did I bring such suffering on myself? Was I too proud of my own work, that this fate fell to me?

I am miserable.

And I am not alone. My other boys resent him too; even the younger ones treat him as the runt. And yet they are afraid, so they torment him. Earlier on, when I was arguing with the Greek about his overpriced ultramarine, I heard them all scrapping in the yard.

'M—,' they cried 'If you are to be a master painter you must perform *all* the tasks you are given! Go now, boy, and find a sieve in which you can bring back a horse's wet shit!'

'Go, M—, a shit in a sieve if you please, master!'

'But I can't sell for any less,' cried the Greek, oblivious to my distraction. 'You will have me on the streets sleeping beneath my stall!'

He waved his fat hands expansively in pseudo-exasperation, my eyes observing two new gold rings on the merchant's fingers. We argued about price rises, import duties, and he was beating me down with sheer loquacity, when M— walked out through the door, a determined look on his face.

Perhaps half an hour later I am teaching – trying to teach – Vitorino to look when he draws. The lad is little better than before; his ineptitude is stubborn to my lessons. We are observing the play of lines in a drapery, soaked in glue and hung over a trestle for their instruction. I am trying to show him how to *see* it, to notice its contours, but also to relish in how lazily it is bathed in the golden light, spilling like syrup from the window, peppered with languid dust, floating like minute angels. I despair of his rendering; I might as well be telling him to draw with his foot.

M— comes trotting in, supporting in his hands and the skirt of his tunic a sieve, purloined God knows where, containing a huge steaming turd. The flies cover his filthy hands, and the absent-minded boy has wiped the sweat from his brow in the day's unforgiving heat, leaving an olive-brown smear across his genial features.

'Master; where does one put the horse-shit?' he asks politely. The boys howl with laughter and roll on the floor – Vito must have summoned them behind my back on M—'s reappearance. They point and jeer, mocking and bullying him as they always do. Even your compatriot Gentle Stephen would retort.

'What are you doing bringing filth into my studio?' I roar, guiltily aware of my intemperate anger, of it's real cause that cannot be hid from heaven or from you who sit there. 'Get rid of it and scrub your hands!

'And you boys! Get to work now or by Lucifer's foul groin the lot of you will be on the street by nightfall! I will not have it said that my pupils have the manners of swine-herders! You, Vitorino! Go with M— and clean the shit from his clothes!'

M— smiles beatifically, puzzled but unworried. He takes no pleasure from the punishment I visit on Vito on his behalf, he takes no umbrage at the trick the boys played on him.

'I'll kill you, you sister fucker!' mutters Vitorino as they head to the trough in the yard, but M— skips around him happily, oblivious to this tough talk. I think of warning the older boy again, but decide not to. I know how the threat of M—, weighing heavily on me, must also affect them. Especially poor dumb Vito.

And you and I both know what that threat is, why they do this to him.

§

Today M— holds the lute in his gentle hands, standing half-naked on a crate. Did I tell you how beautiful he is? The most beautiful amongst them.

Sandro draws him and encourages the boys in their efforts; they stand and sit in a semicircle, tongues out, fingers black with chalk, all drawing their comrade. Sandro is gentler than I – less of the back of his hand and more explanation of their errors. He is a patient and good man, and a good painter. His apprenticeship with me finished two years ago now, but he assists me still whilst getting his name known, finding commissions, and saving to rent his own workshop.

Is it M—'s turn to be the model? Strictly speaking it need not be a matter of turns – I can choose whomsoever I wish, and the boys for the most part are technically only servants; the fastidious Firenze guild prevents me taking more than one official apprentice at a time. Why choose M— to pose? Hmm. I would prefer not to dwell too long on that; certainly I am at greater peace when I know I won't look on one of his drawings at the session's end.

Sandro needs an angel with a lute for the capella fresco. Thank God he is doing that commission. I haven't the strength, the time, nor the inclination. It is under the aegis of my workshop, but they were satisfied for Sandro to work to my design, provided the faces and main figures are of my own hand. Well, I doubt I will bother. They will not check, and it is a

31

stupid stipulation. Everyone knows fresco must be painted before the plaster dries; no use both of us working on the same patch of wall, racing against the warm sun, getting in each other's way. Besides, Sandro's faces are as good as mine to the layman's eye, and those bloody monks know nothing of art.

It is hard to concentrate. A week since I started the predella, and little progression. The boys distract me this afternoon. Maria brings me fresh water, her fat hairy lips kiss the back of my wrinkled neck, and I feel a stirring in my groin as she massages my shoulders. Her wrists are bangled and her fingers beringed like a prostitute's (though woe betide the man who dares insult that fiery woman by suggesting such, now that she's a respectable housemaid). Her dark curly hair is oiled, and her brown skin creased with lines of laughter and sorrow. A woman overflowing with life. She plumps her large backside on a stool beside me, expelling a sigh like a flattened cushion, raises a chubby calf to pick at the corns on her feet, and watches the boys.

'So many boys, Luca! So much mens to cleaning up after and makes foods for! They are supposed being servants, but you let them drawings like apprentice, all of them! They are supposed help me with housework, you know!'

'All right, when they've finished they will be put to their chores. Now I must...'

'I have cleaned all pots, I have sweeping the floor, and makings dinner on my own once again, Luca!'

'Maria my flower, I'm busy! If you could just ... '

She ignores me. 'He is beautiful boy, M—, he helds the lute like a little bambino.'

She babbles on, and I know I will not get a thing done until she goes, so I turn and watch M—. I am not so sure he holds the lute like a baby. Maria, who has never borne children (despite her years 'in the trade' before we met, and our own longstanding affair), tends to see babies everywhere she looks. I, never having been, nor wanting to be, a father, tend to be a bit blind to this obsession of hers. We all see what we want to see in everything.

To my eyes, M— holds the instrument more like a loved one, though I suppose he is too young to know of such passionate embraces. I can't remember how old I was when I collected enough meagre pennies to buy my own first taste of a woman, with the other boys from Master Bernardo's workshop.

M—'s hair is tousled and his cheeks are red with concentration. Every so often he forgets to breathe with focussing so hard, and then his face goes purple. 'Breathe!' shouts Sandro, and the boy gasps for air.

His thin shoulder blades writhe when he yawns or shivers. Sandro will stick wings on those stumps in his drawing. What a crazy thing the imagination of the church is – as if wings would make an angel any more attractive than the glorious figure of a youth. Than this youth.

§

God, but it looks bad! Even the underdrawing seems irredeemable this morning. I have a stinking headache because I got rat-arsed with Bartolomeo yesterday evening, but I was sure it would be atrocious even so. I hate painting today – I hate this god-forsaken scribbling. I have ruined a perfectly good panel. I throw down my brush and the clattering sound reverberates in my skull.

No muse today to guide my hand. Just you and I, Saint and sinner.

Barto says to me last night, in no uncertain terms, that I overreact.

'Don't be so hard on yourself Luca, you whoreson! He's only a boy!'

I tried to concentrate, my head slipping with the wine.

'You don't understand – it's *because* he's only a boy! That's what's so bad! All my work, my lifelong dedication, all my pain – just to be bested by a *kid*!'

'Pain? What pain? Listen to you, you precious old fart! *Everyone* works, *everyone* struggles! What makes you special? You think painters have it worse than anyone else? Try getting halfway through an equestrian statue only to have the commission cancelled! What would *you* do with five tons of drying clay? Let the boy alone! So he has talent; be happy for him!'

'But he surpasses me *now*! What of *my* career?'

'What of it? You're a success you stupid bastard! A good house with your own workshop, no rent to pay, the warmth of a good woman, a string of successful commissions, high standing and respect from your peers – what more do you want for Chrissakes?'

'What about being remembered?'

'Glory and fame are for the fags, the bastard-butcher warlords and the saints, my friend. We makers of beauty should be content *with* making beauty. Screw everlasting life – that's for the priests, Luca. Encourage the boy! If he is to be remembered over you, so be it! Good for him that he comes to a good teacher like you. So be one, you donkey's arsehole!'

Barto slams down his empty beaker. They bring more wine without his asking – as always. Barto's appetite for the vine is justly notorious. I'm sure he is wrong. I was sure last night. Today, with this headache, who knows anything?

I have the drawings before me for the damn portrait of this banker's wife. An ugly old sow, and he stipulates she be painted 'in all her grace and natural beauty.' Idiot. I think I will give this to Sandro too. He could use the experience, and the banker won't ever know – his eye for art is as good as his eye for female grace and beauty. Anyway, my own eyes are like stubborn fish today, swimming away from each other. I will not try to paint more this afternoon.

2

The first wing. The main figure is the Blessed Virgin. A little device of my own; I am centring her so that when the wings of the altarpiece are closed, her face will be level with the Christ in the main panel, her lips ready to kiss his forehead. No one will see it of course, but I like to think I have given her the opportunity to have a precious, unseen moment with the flesh of her own flesh.

I know some months have passed since last we spoke. I also know I am behind schedule. I have found it hard to manage my time; there is just too much to do. And I have to admit (for you know already) that my confidence ebbs, and I've been putting off this work.

§

I am in bed with Maria – not painting now, but still praying. Well, still talking to you, at least. She is chattering on and on endlessly, like a washerwoman. I'm too tired to pay attention, but she's talking more for her own benefit anyway.

All right, so she has a moustache, uncouth manners – she burps and farts publicly without any shame, setting the boys into hysterics – and she speaks like the Sicilian peasant she is. She's more than half a Turk, though she never knew her parents well enough to say which was the infidel; she remembers being called Mariam in her early years, before she took up what she insists on calling the 'Trues Faith'. She is as impressively devout (excepting our sinful living arrangements) as she is extreme in all her passions, and everything else that she does.

But she loves me, and her bosom is massive, big enough to sustain our whole family. I love Maria more tenderly than anything in my life. If I did not have her brown strong arms to fall into, I do not know what would happen to me.

She caught me earlier, speaking to you aloud as I worked, thinking I was alone, with the boys off accompanying Sandro to the market for materials.

'You are madman! Talkings to painting! Lord Almighty, this house *full* of madmans!'

'I'm just talking to myself, just concentrating … '

'Oh! You think I fool?! I tell you I *see* you talks with it!'

'What's wrong with talking to a painting, you stupid woman? St Francis spoke to birds, and I'm not even trying theology!'

'Holy Christ! You compare you to Saints?' She crosses herself in superstitious horror. 'You are stupid man Luca! Stupid stubborn horse-arse!'

How can you argue with such a woman? If I was like virile Barto I would have a new woman every few months; as soon as she became cantankerous I would move on. But I am not, and Maria and I are content to plod along together into old age, as we have for many years already.

I think back to that night in the whorehouse with Barto, a decade ago.

I, too drunk to get it up, and he charging away with the two youngest and prettiest whores there. And I, stuck with a large peasant girl, who repulsed me, singing bawdy songs, cackling like a toothless old crone. But there was something there, something that my drunken and lustful prejudice could not wholly disguise, and before long we were laughing all night, and I fell asleep on her gigantic breasts.

In the morning she led me home to the Corso degli Adimari, and carried me upstairs to my bed. When I awoke, horrendously hung-over, she had tidied the whole house, even ordered the preternaturally messy studio. I am a weak and stupid man, set in my ways. I was, even then. But I saw that I couldn't live without such a woman any longer. My mind was already set, and she never whored that big, brown, buxom and, above all, beautiful body again. I love her dearly.

There are two images in Maria's room. One is a quite poor picture of my own; one of the ready-made lines I do for the tasteless public, depicting John the Baptist. The other is a drawing of M—'s. I try hard not to look at it when we go to sleep.

§

I watch the boy's hand glide over the surface, without hesitation, gracefully, like an experienced lover plying the trade of his fingers to a woman's body. His touch is firm or light, but always exact; rarely does he change a line, though often many will coalesce, successive additions softening and dispelling, or conversely, exaggerating, a contour.

The surface becomes dense. It writhes with tones and patterns of formless matter, then before your eyes they begin to link up. His hand like a spider spinning a web, but around a form it has already caught. Faces emerge, gradually, wearing such expression you almost talk to them. If the boy ever draws grapes he will put Apelles himself to shame. You could swear that his drapery will move in the breeze.

From shadow he brings forth form, from light he returns to shadow. I have never seen such worked drawing. He darkens the paper all over so that the surface seems to have disappeared, and what you are staring into has all the volume of the image on a fine mirror.

When he steps back from the easel the little gathering of painters, sculptors and craftsmen in my workshop let out a collective sigh. There before us lies a piece of the world, frozen, monochromatic, and yet real. The boy has made little effort to hide his marks; the lines and smudges, the patches from which the drawing is made. Yet somehow that adds to the charm. Several people clap him on the back, praise the drawing briefly, but mostly they are silent. A low buzz of conversation starts up only as M— leaves at my instigation to wash the charcoal from his face and hands.

Barto speaks first. 'That, friends, is a talent and more.'

'Honestly, have you ever seen anything like this?'

'Before today I would not have believed such talent could exist in a child.'

'You have taught him this, Luca?' asks Matteo the painter.

'I wish that I had! He's had the same lessons as the others, but his technique is his own. He draws all the time. He is like an ox ploughing a furrow; he just keeps at it and at it.'

'Then where did he learn it?'

'When they were publicly displayed, he was obsessed with the drawings of the Genius of Vinci and Master Buonarroti – not that that explains his own innate ability.' I add gloomily.

'If it were not a sin I would say the boy's Christ puts Lentulus's account to shame!' says Barto, arms folded across his powerful chest.

'His name will eclipse us all; you are lucky to be the one to bring him forth, Luca.'

I do not see who utters these words. They pain me like blows to my chest. What – am I to be grateful for *that*?

3

The second wing; the painting of you, my namesake and intercessor. I'm afraid to approach the Virgin, let alone Christ. Truthfully, I neither understand, nor can bear to face, the idea of God. But I do not worry myself, as long as I can talk to you. As long as you are there, I have someone to talk for me, for if you are with them at all – if *they* are there at all – you understand them better than I can hope to. You, my reflection, but a reflection without the flaws and failings etched into my own face.

I am even (forgive me this blasphemous idiosyncrasy) modelling your features, perhaps a little, on my own.

You will have been painting Mary in my image. If it were really your work on the easel I have put behind you, it would be incomparably greater than my rendering. Sometimes I wonder if you ever saw her. It seems to me that the more uncertainty we have, the more we need paintings, and the more paintings there are of something, the more uncertain we must be about it. There are so many depictions of you painting her. Are we uncertain of you, or do we perhaps see how uncertain you might have been, as a mortal, fallible man? Did you have your own trials of faith? Did you have to paint her for your own sanity, to keep your own belief?

§

Barto and I sit together, drinking wine again. His rough unshaven face beneath his curly unkempt hair is engraved with serious lines – his thoughts are with the piece sitting in his workshop, his mind working on it now, even as I am thinking of you and the altarpiece.

I like being around Barto when he is like this; frowning façade of a face supported by his powerful fists, the sinews and muscles bulging in those forearms with their coating of marble dust, matting the forest of hairs. He is starting to lose the hair on his crown, and the sunburnt tip of his head is as smooth and polished as the cheek of one of his stone saints. He is rough and dirty from the day's work, his clothes grey with dust. He draws an arm on the tablecloth with a charcoal twig, endlessly and from different angles. I can see he's having trouble.

We sit in silence. Moments before we were arguing about Alberti's treatise, which a bibliophile patron of his showed him recently. Suddenly I fear Barto's concentration, that it is more devout than mine, makes him a worthier artist, and quickly I resurrect the subject.

'I still say that a man who writes a book defining a subsequent manner of painting, a manner still preoccupying painters now, *is* a visionary.'

Barto shakes his head gruffly, relieving himself from the half-formed marble block he's struggling with, and returning to the debate.

'*Only because* painters and their patrons wanted such paintings in the manner he describes. People moved away from gold leaf, preferred fewer but significant actors in their *istoria* rather than confusing crowds. So you think this Alberti ... prophetic, almost. But it could have been different; other painters, in the future maybe, now they –'

'But he wrote it a *century* ago Barto, and it's *still* –'

'Fuck when he wrote it! All that matters is *how* people do things, not some big false 'why' imposed afterwards. Maybe the next fashion will be flat, precious surfaces again, discarding perspective – or maybe not. But I'm not saying Alberti was *wrong* about what developed – only that it's not 'prophecy'. He just said what he liked. You can never say for certain how art will end up – history comes about afterwards; you don't *know* where it will go before it's happened.'

'But he *did*! You're ignorant Barto; stupid and ignorant. You drink till your brain is soused and then you spout off like a mother-in-law! The world goes according to God's plan, and has a pattern! Now – '

'And I'm not saying there *isn't* a pattern! But history has nothing to do with that. History is what men do when they look backwards. Look; has God's plan told you what clothes to wear today, or did your Sicilian mistress lay them out for you? Your trouble is your head is off looking for ethereal mysteries, Luca. I am *here*, on the earth, doing things with my hands,' he shakes his strong fists at me, 'you need to stay in reality my friend, make the most of it. Stop flitting away; you aren't some poet trying to comprehend the divine – you're better than that. You're a man of craft!'

We carry on, more and more drunkenly, the argument getting so heated we are shouting at each other, and suddenly I'm lurching away, going home in a terrible sulk. Fall through the front door into the workshop. Manage to light a lamp; so drunk, but too wound-up for sleep. Start looking – I don't know why – through my drawings, for the altarpiece.

Furious with them, with myself, with you even, yes you. You should be helping me, holding me up.

Fatal – know I shouldn't, but doing it anyway; start looking at M—'s drawings. Piled on the shelf next to mine. Sandro saved up, bought him extra paper, can you believe that? He's a kind man, wants to see just how good the boy is. Sifting through them, can't focus on individual ones, all intertwining, mixing up, and hit me like cold water, like a sobering blow:

Swathes of dark velvet charcoal cloak the paper, impenetrable curtains of refined plasticity blanking and blocking the penetrating eye. But through chinks in the dusk the greedy consumptive gaze feasts on flesh, flesh of such beauty and rawness, haunches and shoulders, scrawny neck and solid leg. Muscles ripple and bulge, like taut springs ready to snap, meat to be incised with sharp teeth, its stark and shocking life ebbing into the void under the playful chiaroscuro. These limbs, half-succumbed already to the voracious leprosy of the umbra, half-illuminated by antiquarian light, always burgeoning on the point of release and ecstasy, always a fraction of a moment from movement.

These parts, dismembered by the dark, fuse and trace forms behind the blackness, suddenly a patch of shadow buried in profounder shade resolves into the jowl and cheek of an unseen face, figures materialise, from nothing, their genesis swathed in a begetting sensuality. Delicate, astounding sfumato blending forms into each other and into the darkness. Gesture sears trails across the gloomy abyss between thigh and bicep, meaning skims across the discontinuous surface and it begins to cohere, fractured pools of light unifying and running together.

(My fingers crumple into the paper, salt tears stab my eyes, I pull away, teeter up the stairs – the pictures don't leave my head…)

As torsos gather life, frozen and postponed but ineradicable, as fingers clutch with the vice-like strength of animal energy, blood boils below the surface-sheen, skin registers the pulse of empowered hearts. Cloth that restricts and shrouds limbs is torn, rent by the spillage of flesh, the libidinous tease of a charged and futile sexuality on display, an epidermis of desire even in the stocky ruggedness of a repellent old man, the labial folds of an ancient woman's face, the straining, veined shoulder of a Herculean youth, the promising mouth of the seductive Salome, a wound compelling to the touch. Eyes like jewels hidden beneath grey sacks of lids, drooping shadows that obscure all but a dark slit, until the toss of a head, the turn of a neck, the raising of a face, unleashes such a glare, such a piercing glassy brightness – marbles that entice magpies as much as corneas that beckon crows.

(Crash onto the spinning bed, Maria starts, asks me something, she's holding my face...can't focus on her eyes...my head slams into the headboard...)

These ruddy and flaccid, sensuous and sculptured, fundamentally flawed people live between the light and the dark, committed to neither, ruled only by the anchors of tactile sense, of touch and taste, smell and sound. Their passage between inscrutable shade and illumination is not for their own apprehension; their display is unwitting and unwilling.

Tell me, fucking tell me: how does such a naïve, gangling, simple boy make work like this?

(Burying into the blanket, into Maria, into despair. Will you not free me from him? Will you not...?)

4

He has drawn it for me! By all that is unholy *he has drawn it!* I come down this morning, depressed, yet resigned to struggle again with the head of the Christ that has been preventing me from continuing the main panel for three weeks, and the boy just so happens to have left out a drawing for me, a head in exactly the right position, exactly the right turn to match the body. He has drawn it on the verso of one of my rejected early attempts. Does he do it to spite me? No, he's too innocent for that. But the rage, the anger in me now...

And the worst of it is, it even looks slightly like him! I have often noted how artists will unthinkingly apply their own features to those of their subject, and he has done precisely that. The Christ could be him, in a few years, with a light, almost downy beard. It is the most beautiful head of Jesus I have ever seen.

Such fury has taken me. But I cannot destroy it; I need this drawing. I do not have time to waste on more failed attempts. It is already more than two months since the panel of you was completed.

§

41

Oh but do I have to go over it again? I pray for forgiveness, and in doing so return constantly to my sin. Must I repeat what already tortures me?

§

I come into my workshop, feel a wave of tremulous nausea at the tone of the boys' cries and shouts, taste and feel the sweet-sour shock of violence. I am appalled and repelled, slightly afraid, as if entering the lair of some beast. All of this I feel in an instant.

A fight is taking place. I stride in, pull the spectating boys aside, and in the middle of the floor is Vito, grim determination and hatred on his face as he holds M— in a headlock. Blood flows from M—'s nose, tears from his eyes. He howls in pain and fright. I grab Vito's shoulder roughly and instantly he shoves M— away, as if nothing's happened, but the boy has no sense of balance and trips, knocking a table. A porphyry slab covered in neat piles of ground pigment crashes to the floor, cracks in half, coloured powder sprays all over the painting of the banker's wife leaning against the wall, as does a pot of oil, also descending from the table.

'What have you done?' I scream, rage filling me and overflowing, carrying me like a downstream current.

'He was beating me!' snivels M—.

'He started it!' cries Vito hotly.

Now of course I know where blame lies, I know what I should do, who is to be punished.

But rage and jealousy do strange things to the mind, to the judgement, to the soul.

§

In the dark streets drunk men shout, dogs chase each other's barks with howls of their own. But that is all a background susurrus, a nothing, a void, compared to the timid knocking at the shutters of the ground floor windows, the thin little voice calling words I try not to hear with the pillow wrapped around my head.

I have made them sleep in the woodshed in the yard. To teach them. Nothing but a thin blanket each. No supper. They must respect a workshop or they are not fit to be in one.

It is raining now. Again the tapping from downstairs, the scared little voice calling 'Master?' over and over. Crying that it is cold and wet.

It rains harder. After an age the voice and tapping stop, but not in my head.

Will he never let me be?

§

M— has a fever. I am distraught. I cannot work. The physician says he is very sick. Perhaps he will not recover. I cannot paint.

§

Eight days he has been in bed now. I climb the stairs to the loft, open the door, timorous with guilt and the fear of death. I look down at the boy and my chest aches unbearably. His face is white, his eyes stare at nothing, darting from side to side, yellow-rimmed. When he coughs the sound is like water gurgling through a pipe.

Maria mops his brow, leaning from the dark shadows by his bed into the shaft of light falling across his chest and throat. She has sat there day and night. The stark contrast of light and shade makes me think of the boy's work, of how he would render her. She looks up at me and I see puffy red rings of flesh around those silent but accusatory Sicilian eyes. Tears muffle my sight and prick me, and I have to leave.

§

The third week since…

None of the boys speak to me, they avert their eyes when they meet me. Shuffle around silently. The workshop is dead, but for the rats.

All have gone to see him, taken him little gifts. Even Vito has cried for him. The physician says it's close now. I can no longer bear to visit him. I haven't for five days. Food is tasteless, water quenches nothing, and this bloody altarpiece is beyond my capacity. For days all I have done is stare hopelessly at it.

§

You bastard! YOU FUCKING, FUCKING BASTARD! Why have you *done* this to me? What did I do to deserve this?

I stumble melodramatically in the rain, through empty streets alone. Maria wraps me in a blanket when I return, makes me a hot glass of wine. She says nothing.

I hate you! I HATE YOU!

5

Is Barto right; is history only made afterwards? The boy will never grace history now, and that seems wrong for such a sublime talent. Then was there a pattern, was M— meant to have lived, and achieved the great things he was clearly destined for? But how could God's will be challenged by what we do?

Perhaps there is nothing *but* what we do, what we have done.

Either way I seem to find no consolation, and I deserve none, as I am sure you would tell me.

My only hope is that others will come, others who have his skill, who will make the discoveries he made. Others who can dash the fame of our generation, wrest from us the torch, and carry on with it into the night. The hope that I have not ruined forever something that was beautiful, something that men deserved to see. It is a small hope, but it is all I have.

The Confraternity is happy with the work. Cries of admiration when it was installed, mostly for the head of Christ.

There were some criticisms too, expressions of concern about the male

44

Saint's face, murmurs that he looked like a sinner, a haunted, desperate man. So be it. May those who look on him always know that the depicted figure needs all the prayers he can get.

My completed altarpiece, in situ. Its crowning glory, a face that was not of my own hand.

Seen in the gathering gloom the work as a whole looks better than perhaps it is, and reminds me of M—'s drawings, its swathes of shadow and bathing streams of luminosity exacerbated by the mysterious half-light in the church. God's nature, His day and night, give my work a value it does not ordinarily have. And as my picture now fades into the candlelit twilight, as its completion slips away into darkness, so my prayer, my guilt, my woe and tale of sin, I hope, can hide in obscurity; if my fame is to be eclipsed by young progressives, so – I can hope – will my private infamy. The darkness takes and conceals that which will never be revealed, and you, Saint Luke, disappear into the dusk of the church with the others.

Russian Tea

Emma Darwin

It wasn't the great ones who came into Mikhail's dreams that night. Not the ones he'd wept for, not Arkhangelsk, who he knew to be a miracle at the first thrust of his wet forelegs among the straw. Not Baba Yaga, who'd cost him the vet four times before she was a yearling, and then suddenly grew and toughened and raced, and then dropped him more winners of her own than any other mare he'd bred. Not Little Peter, with his tail like a silk pennant, and his Barbary blood, and the exquisite, disdainful curve to his face.

No, it was the middling ones, the ones that he'd give a chance to, a chance to show they had some speed or cleverness or courage or mere brute strength. A chance – a couple of chances – and then if they didn't have quite enough of whatever it was, he sold them on, because he had to. Their names he had all but forgotten, flickering into his memory and snuffing out again. But it was they who walked through his sleep that night, one after the other, a long, expensive string, a rope tying every part of that life together. And the smell of them, like red wine that's been left in the sun, the deep, sharp smell of animal, of fur and sweat. He would put his nose to it and be drunk in an instant, in love with the swell of warm muscle, with the shiver and twitch of the satin skin, with the liquid-dark eye, always alive with the ancestral memory of wolves.

That smell lingered in his mind, even when he sat up and pushed back the blankets, and took a waking breath of new rain outside and old damp within, and the oil stove, and last night's cabbage soup. Only a little of the light that fell between the area railings dribbled through the bald patches in the plush curtains. Rather than use electricity to dress by he opened them, judging the temperature by the quality of the light, for it was always cold in his room, a subterranean chill that wavered each time an underground train rumbled under the lino, and then settled again.

Shaving cost hot water, but he couldn't bring himself not to, any more than he could once have brought himself to leave a bridle stiffened with melted snow, or a horse's belly dirty and chafed with girth sweat. If all the lads were busy – properly busy, as ordered – then he'd do it himself. He might still be at it when the Count dropped by to see how his stud was getting on that morning. The Count didn't mind; he was probably finding time a little heavy on his hands, while his coach took his mistress to the railway station for the St. Petersburg train and waited to pick up the Countess, his wife. He just nodded to Mikhail, and leant on the box door and talked of hunting and breeding, until the bridle was soft and glossy, or the horse comfortable.

Sometimes Mikhail would walk to Piccadilly and save the Tube fare. It was easier than squeezing his pack and himself into the lift at Gloucester Road Station. Today was quite bright after the rain, and warm for October. The city pavements didn't change with weather or season, except from dark to pale, and back, but by noon the going would have dried out to soft. If he walked he could stop in Green Park, and dig his heel into the beaded grass and damp earth, and judge it for himself. But a little of his strength seemed to have stayed with the horses in his dreams, and he crossed Cromwell Road and queued at the ticket office, and then sank with all the others in their dark coats, down the lift shaft into the black, rattling dryness of the Tube.

His pitch was by St James's Church. Yellow sunlight was scraping past the square stones of the tower and striping the pavement. No one was there to be sent away, and Mikhail set down his pack, shifted it till it was steady and put on his money belt. Then he unfolded the tray on the top and got out his stock.

He set out pencils, shoe polish, gaspers, sets of buttons, packs of thin playing cards, a few pairs of glass earrings, two packets of dominoes, and between them on the upper shelf, one of the necklaces of artificial pearls. It looked well there in its open box, but nobody ever asked for it, and he regretted buying two.

After that, he stood.

When he had first stood there, he had looked about him, trying to see

48

customers, trying to catch their eye and draw their attention to his goods. The thick, post-war drabness was even then being cracked apart from within. People wanted to find things to enjoy, to buy, to have something new that didn't remind them of the past, and of death. But slowly he learned to untwist the English he heard, and spelt out the news in papers he picked up from the gutter, and then he saw the cracks for what they really were: the streets unlit and the dark mass of miners filling the city; arrests in the East End, Communist meetings, shootings, hangings, hunger strikes in Ireland. More and more he feared that he'd been foolish to come to London. Had he taken his one chance, had he lived through train journeys as endless as nightmares, dark checkpoints, nameless stations, police, soldiers, false flimsy papers, and hunger and fear gnawing in his belly every day and night... had he survived, when so many had not, only to find it happening here, too? Those cracks reminded him too much of the very beginnings of it all in St. Petersburg, of the days when the attics and basements and steamed-up cafés finally split open, and spewed out the hotheads and the anarchists. Out in the streets there had always been raw anger, lying like dirty late-winter snow, and as the two met they melted together into a flood. Even now, Mikhail sometimes had to reassure himself that here in England the anger never lasted, and revolutionary speeches were smothered by the fog. Here, a man might hope to sleep.

A pair of brown bootlaces? Threepence, please, sir. The customer took them, nodded, and moved on, pocketing the change from his shilling. As if Mikhail had suddenly become visible several more people stopped, and he sold a few things, although one stout woman couldn't match her lost button to her satisfaction from his stock, and an elderly man berated him briefly for selling cigarettes made in Virginia. Did he have any idea of the conditions in which they were made? Mikhail thought he was saying, or something like it. The tone was familiar, anyway. Mikhail had thrown out a stable lad once, who'd tried to persuade the others they were exploited, or they were lackeys to the oppressors – Mikhail had never bothered to find out which – or anything except what they were, stupid peasant lads who were clever with horses and worked hard for a roof and their keep and a wage. He'd given the lad a warning, and the next time he heard him spilling out silly, dangerous talk in the sweet-smelling hayloft, handed him his week's money and had two of the foresters run him off the estate.

'I said, how much are the cards?'

'I beg pardon, sir,' said Mikhail, and dragged his mind back from the larch woods. 'Very good quality, ninepence.'

The man turned them over with a frown. 'Give you sixpence.'

Mikhail sighed. They cost him fivepence, but it would be a little less to carry home.

'Done.'

'Ta,' said the man, and dropped the money into his hand and went off.

The pavements were emptying. Anyone going to work was late, and it was too early for the shoppers. As the chances of selling anything slackened Mikhail felt himself solidifying inside his coat. It was still good, even where he'd mended the rent in the back after he'd caught it on the coupling as he scrambled between two railway trucks at Pskov. Now it was like a shell inside which he settled into a kind of thick stillness, like the stillness of a horse standing under a tree, one hind leg hitched up, eyes closed, and the whisk of its tail the only movement, the only acknowledgement of its being a living thing.

To Elena, the pedlar might have been made of the same grubby old stone as the pillar he stood in front of, until she saw the dominoes. She had meant to get a present for Mrs. Donovan's grandson. He was coming to tea in the kitchen that afternoon for his birthday – Mrs. Donovan had asked if he might – and Elena had forgotten, and now here was just the thing. She stopped.

'How much are the dominoes?' They wouldn't be dear: the box was crudely painted and flimsy but the boy wouldn't mind, perhaps he'd be pleased, and Mrs. Donovan would forgive her for muddling the baker's order this morning.

'One shilling.'

She shook the coins about in her purse and found a florin. Dropping it into the dark-stained leather of his palm, she looked up and, from somewhere inside the past, came a name.

'M Filippov?'

'Mme. Vershinsky!' He lifted his hat to her, and for a second she almost fancied she could see the slanting, brilliant light of the summers outside St. Petersburg peeping through the lines of his face.

'When did you come to England?' he said in French. 'Is M Vershinsky here?'

'He died,' she said in Russian. 'In Paris.' For a moment she saw the attic in Montmartre and heard Andrei coughing. Then she went on, 'I've married again – I'm Mrs. Brownlow now. My husband's a doctor here. And you?'

'I got out in 1918,' he said, also in Russian. 'I couldn't bring anything with me. This is – this work is a stopgap.'

'Where are you living?'

'I have a room in a little street called Emperor's Gate, near Cromwell Road.'

'But I live in Cornwall Gardens!' she cried, feeling that she'd made some great discovery, some connection that would resolve everything. 'Just round the corner!'

'Excuse me,' said a dry, scratchy, English voice. Elena stepped aside. 'Have you any pencils harder than HB?'

M Filippov started to look through the box and Elena watched, seeing the worn elbows of his coat and his cracked and carefully polished boots, hearing his English, which was more fluent than hers, but not so correct. It was quite warm; the fur collar of her own coat was only rabbit, but it was hot about her neck.

Then another customer came along, and another. It was getting on for lunchtime M Filippov said, and that made her realise that she hadn't finished her shopping. There was still Swan & Edgar to do, and she was going to be late for lunch. Mrs. Donovan would be disapproving, though Edward probably wouldn't notice, or at least say anything. She bought the dominoes and said good bye, and hurried away.

When her bus came growling up to the stop she got on and climbed upstairs, a little awkward with all her parcels, and sat with the tired, yellowing leaves of the plane trees in the park almost brushing her shoulder as she was borne past, the wind of movement catching at her hat. After Hyde Park Corner the trees were on the far side of the road.

As ever, Edward asked about how she had spent her morning, but as ever he was too preoccupied with his patients – with what he could do for those he could help, what he must say to those he could not – to talk a great deal to her. As they were drinking their coffee, though, he said suddenly that they would be entertaining more, now that his FRSM had come through; he would increase her housekeeping allowance, of course. 'And you must feel free to spend some of it on yourself, my dear,' he said. 'No doubt you will need some new things for the winter.' Elena nodded and thanked him, and wished there was something she could say to Mrs. Donovan that would make the coffee drinkable. Edward didn't seem to mind it; indeed, he asked for another cup, but he finished it quickly, and went off to start his house calls.

In the afternoon there were bills to pay, laundry lists to make up, the flowers for the waiting room and the hall. Elena worked her way through it all, trying not to hear the laughter from the kitchen. When she went in with her present there was a cake, and candles waiting to be lit, and the little boy was pulling the paper off a parcel, but they didn't want her there. They stood politely, Mrs. Donovan with her hands folded in front of her apron as if she were taking the day's orders, and the little boy – Walter, his name turned out to be – blushing, with his mother's hand gripped into his shoulder. He seemed to like the dominoes, and they thanked her, and waited for her to go.

After dinner Edward went back down to the surgery and Elena got out her mending basket and switched on the wireless because it was good for her English, and when she felt chilly, the electric fire. But it was Russian she heard in her mind, as warm and near as if it were being spoken in the next room, and as she dipped her needle in and out of the lisle of one of her winter stockings, spanning the hole over and over with the thread until it was closed, it seemed as if the voices lifted things from her memory and spilt them into her lap on top of the greyness. Bronze-coloured trees with their leaves shivering; an embroidered shawl flung onto the grass, long windows with muslin blinds; cherries, cold vodka, roast salmon; their friends arguing about Palladio, Picasso, Lloyd Wright, Marx; the white summer river-light still rippling at midnight across the ceiling of her father's flat on the Neva. The endless day had seemed to soak into the rooms so that even in winter the sun was still with them. When anyone opened the door of the stove the red and yellow heat thrust into the room like a great tiger paw, seizing the offered larch logs, before the door was shut and the stove once more crouched quietly in the corner of the room.

When Edward came upstairs it was quite late and she was already in bed, but he was not as tired as she'd thought he would be after a busy day. Afterwards, feeling his breathing settle into sleep against her back, she let her thoughts run back to Russia. The Count's stud, that was where she had first met M Filippov. Andrei had been summoned out from St. Petersburg to discuss re-building the old part of the house, and suggested that she come too, that they make a day of it. The Count had been charming, taking her hand and smiling. She was still trying to bring the memories close enough to step into, when she fell asleep.

'And what are you up to today, my dear?' Edward asked, leaning over her as he knotted his tie in the dressing table mirror. The day wasn't as bright as yesterday, and she'd had to switch on the light above it, but at least with the coal strike over they no longer had to save electricity.

'Only ordinary things,' said Elena.

Edward's hands stilled and he met her eyes in the mirror. 'You are all right, aren't you, my dear? You will say if there is anything I can do, won't you?'

'Of course I'm all right,' she said, looking down.

He finished tying his tie and went down to the dining room, and though he liked her to pour his tea for him, for a moment she sat on in front of her mirror. What she had said was true: she was all right – warm, fed, clothed, not frightened or ill – and it was Edward who had found her, and brought her to such safety.

By eleven o'clock she was walking round the corner into Emperor's Gate.

The street was longer than she'd realised; it doubled back on itself. How on earth was she going to find where he lived? She couldn't just stand there, and he wasn't likely to come home at this hour. People might think things; it was rather that sort of street. She'd had enough of that – of men who thought that – in Montmartre. Even when she had her arms full of stained linen someone might step too close, say something, loom over her.

Even the time when she stumbled down the stone stairs, driven by the endless coughing, and ran along the street to fetch the doctor. She'd sworn at the man in Russian, and pushed past him, with blood and sputum spattered all down her shabby muslin frock.

None of that now, she told herself. There wasn't any need to swear now, or anything else. She would walk once round, and then go up to Barker's for the dishcloths Mrs. Donovan had asked for.

She saw M Filippov trudging round the angle at the furthest point of Emperor's Gate. He was bent under the weight of his pack, but when she held out her hand he straightened a little and raised his hat, so that there flickered across her memory a ghost of him, striding easily towards a horse that baulked and tossed its head in fear. As soon as he grasped its bridle, the horse stepped through the gate like a stream of silk. But now she didn't know what to say.

Mikhail felt her silence, but couldn't read it. It was like that time in the Caucasus, buying horses. They had celebrated the bargain with a meal, sitting round the great fire that flared into the dry mountain air, and he had been offered a place in the stamping, clapping dance that was starting up. He had no idea what the steps were; should he refuse, or make a fool of himself by trying to dance?

Eventually he gave her a slight bow, like an army officer, and said, 'I have only one room, Mme. Brownlow, or I would offer you some tea.'

How silly she had been, Elena realised. It had been silly to come, to walk so slowly past all the sooty railings, looking for his name above the bakelite doorbells, silly to be so pleased when she saw it in the shadow of the area doorway, the small card pinned with an ordinary drawing pin that was now a little rusty. The script was small too, but Russian, thick with its spikes and loops: Mikhail Petrovich Filippov.

But before she could bring herself to say goodbye to him he said, 'On the other hand, there is a café near here – do you know it? – run by Russians. Well, Ukrainians, from Kiev, but still – If you would care to wait for a moment while I put my things away? They serve proper tea.'

'I had no idea there was such a place,' she said. She had never dared to try teaching Mrs. Donovan to make Russian tea, nor even known where to buy it, and her mouth and her stomach suddenly ached with desire. 'I'd love to go there.'

The café was the last shop along the side of South Kensington Station. Beyond it, Elena saw, the white, elaborate houses were ranged round a square garden. That's all that's left of nature for Londoners, she thought in Andrei's voice. Those who can afford to buy it and rail it off and lock out everyone else, clinging to a scrap of private countryside in their interminable city. Of course they cling to it, her own voice answered in her head. It's all they have to remind them. It's where they'd rather be.

'I don't know if it will be busy,' Mikhail said, as they approached. 'I usually come in the evenings.' He was as conscious of the single ten shilling note in the breast pocket of his coat as he had once been of the thick wads of roubles he kept there for the bookies, for the gate men, for a lad who did well or an official who might otherwise decide badly. This morning he had sold both the necklaces to the same man, and though he'd come home meaning to spend the money on the pretty little Armenian tart with the white teeth who lived on the corner, he was suddenly glad to spend it instead on Mme. Brownlow, who was well dressed, and lived in one of the big houses that his backed on to, but who was thin and pale and spoke Russian uncertainly. She even hesitated a little when she walked, like a horse turned out to grass for the first time in years.

The café was quiet, with only one couple who he didn't know in the far corner. He asked her what she would like. A glass of tea would be lovely, she said. He went on, in the expansiveness of having money, 'And would you care for something to eat? Some *kulich*, perhaps?'

She hesitated, while she pulled off her gloves, and then said, 'No, thank you, tea is plenty.'

'I have a snack myself at this hour, generally,' he said, knowing suddenly that she was trying to save him money, that she had guessed that his snack was, generally, a swig from his water bottle, with a little vodka in it on cold days. 'They have a cherry tart which is almost as good as you could get in St. Petersburg.'

The waitress set their tea down in front of them, and its scent rose: fruit, lemons and new-mown hay, just as it should. Did it come from Russia? Elena asked, in Russian. The waitress smiled with bad teeth: no, they got their tea in Whitechapel, she said, there were several places there, mostly run by Jews of course, Whitechapel was like that. But there was nothing wrong with the tea.

As they drank, M Filippov seemed to straighten and fill out again, asking the waitress how the family were, making a joke about news of one of them who had emigrated to America. And yes, he would be seeing Ivan, and could give him a message. Elena wondered who Ivan was, and where M Filippov would see him, and how soon, and then found that she had agreed after all to have something to eat.

'The grandmother was half-English,' he said, when the waitress had gone. 'They had family over here when they got out.'

Elena thought of Andrei's sister in Paris. How shocked Nina was that she and Andrei had taken their chance to leave St. Petersburg! She was eager only for news that might mean that she could go back, that the pale mill girls and half-blind lace-makers she had tried to help and who could not help her when the Tsar's police came, would now be her passport home. She never quite said that Andrei would not have got ill if they'd stayed, that any day now the cold and the hunger would have retreated from his bones and blood and let him get well. She never quite said it, but she wrote from Moscow of Party members full of health and good spirits at the triumph of the People's Will.

The café windows were misting over inside, as if the fumes that rose from the opal-coloured, gleaming tea in its glass and gilt, were veiling it from the uncomprehending gaze of the English passers-by. Even if they bothered to look in they would not understand the faded photographs on the walls. There were turbans and sleighs and camels and mosques, dark Mongolian eyes glinting from the door of a tent, ponies tethered in the snow. Such things had been part of her life, Elena thought: you could see them in the marketplace or from a train window. Here in England they were flat little engravings in story books and encyclopaedias. Only one photograph, for a moment, might seem familiar, for the Tsar in his braided uniform had been the spit of his still-living cousin, their own King. The Tsaritsa and her daughters looked English and old-fashioned too, all bustles and pinafores and flowery hats. But the Tsarevich's high-necked, belted Russian smock and breeches gave the game away, betrayed the snow, the fire, the foreignness; that, and knowing that somewhere in snow or fire lay their broken bodies.

Mikhail guessed that the waitress had cut a new cherry tart specially for them; the fruit was plump and the pastry crisp. They ate and sipped tea and talked of St. Petersburg, and Paris, and Mme. Brownlow's cheeks grew pink. He had a sudden fancy that the cherry juice itself was running through her veins and suffusing her skin.

'M Filippov – '

'Please, you must call me Mikhail Petrovich.'

The Russian name was right for him, she thought, or for anyone: not simple but plain, no subservient Russian title or fashionable French one, no shiny new comradeship, not even a family name to keep him in his place. Simply his christening name, and his father's, given, and kept forever. She smiled. 'Mikhail Petrovich, then. And you must call me Elena Nicolaevna.'

He smiled in his turn. 'Elena Nicolaevna,' he said, and suddenly she was stabbed with longing for Andrei, for home, for everything that was gone, and a small despair welled up in her throat and spilt out before she could stop it.

'Are you all right?' he said, putting out his hand towards her.

She fumbled in her sleeve for her handkerchief and blew her nose, which often worked, and it did this time, so she was able to say, 'Yes, I'm fine. It's… I haven't been called that for so long. It reminded me, that's all. I'm sorry to be so silly.'

'I know. I do not use Petrovich, except with my Russian friends. Russian names seem to confuse the English.'

She said suddenly, 'At least, at home, I had that, even when I was married. I was always Elena Nicolaevna.'

Mikhail had never thought of that. As he gestured to the waitress for more tea, he thought of the women he'd had affairs with. They'd been married already or between husbands, and the rest of the time he'd picked up girls who didn't belong to anyone. He'd had no desire to be married himself, nor even to keep a woman, though as he rose in the world he could have afforded it well enough. What, with fifty horses in the yard? he'd say when the subject came up. No, thank you, he had quite enough beautiful, temperamental creatures to coddle as it was. And the ladies at the table would laugh as much as the men did. Even now he could almost smell the women's perfume. Often he recalled those evenings just so that he might not see these grey streets and dark rooms for a few moments. But suddenly he wondered if the women had been laughing at the same joke.

Elena saw the flicker of puzzlement in his eyes, and wondered if he had been married, as the fresh tea scalded its way down her throat like *eau-de-vie*. She could not recall mention of a wife, and he had said nothing of one today. Yet he had been an attractive man, with confidence about him; not Andrei's sudden brilliance but the steady glow of strength, of physical competence. Now he was older, poorer, but there was something still there, she saw suddenly, some of that glow, something that made her memories of Andrei, and St. Petersburg, and her father more than just faded photographs, made them swell and breathe. Might that breathing warm her now, let her grow into something alive?

She stretched her back and looked about her. Above the till was a clock, and it said a quarter to one. Her wristwatch said the same.

'Oh, my goodness!' She leapt to her feet and snatched up her gloves. 'I'd no idea it was that late! I must go!'

He got up immediately and caught the waitress's eye. 'Of course. You must forgive me for having kept you.'

'Oh no, no, I wish I could stay!' she said wildly, unnerved by the possibility of Mrs. Donovan's anger, and Edward's legitimate questions. She pulled herself together. 'That is, thank you so much for the tea.'

'It's been a pleasure,' he said, and drew on his gloves. He fished a ten-shilling note out of his pocket and paid the bill so casually, without glancing at it, that it was a moment before she remembered her first sight of him, standing by the sooty pillar of St James's. Only then did she wonder how often he had such an amount to spend on tea and cakes, or could afford a morning away from his stand.

'Are you going back to Cornwall Gardens?' he asked as he held the café door for her. 'May I escort you?'

'Of course,' she said. He settled his hat and they walked back along Stanhope Gardens and up Gloucester Road, talking of the weather and the shops, just for the pleasure, she felt, of speaking their own language.

58

At the corner of Cornwall Gardens Mikhail stopped. 'Perhaps we should say goodbye here,' he said, holding out his hand. She took it, and through the gap in her tightly buttoned gloves he could feel a pulse beating in her wrist. It seemed to him suddenly that if he could hold it for long enough – that little swell of life under his fingers – then he might again be able to live as he once had, beyond this drudgery for food and fire, strong enough to wake easily at dawn, command men and horses, make money and spend it, drink, hunt and sleep sound.

She let go. 'Thank you for everything,' she said, and then, 'I hope we meet again.'

He smiled. 'I hope so too.' Then he made her a little bow as he lifted his hat, and walked away.

She watched him for a moment, and then started along the pavement towards her house. The butcher's boy brushed past her on his bicycle, the back wheel catching at the hem of her coat, and she swore at him in Russian. At the foot of the steps, with her latchkey already in her hand, she stopped, turned, and walked back towards Gloucester Road Station.

She would telephone from Whitechapel, and let Mrs. Donovan and Edward know that she would not be in for lunch.

Dreamed a Dream

Judy Crozier

We were homeward bound one night on the deep

Swingin' in my hammock, I fell asleep

I dreamed a dream, and I thought it true

Concernin' Franklin and his gallant crew

Lord Franklin. Anon.

A vast silence that swallows these tiny lives of ours. It cannot be broken by the creaking of the ice or the lonely bark of a seal. The creak, the bark, the hoarse cough of a miserable sailor, all sucked into the dead weight of silence that lies over us all. Silence as great as the ice that has our two ships fast, and as the sight of the ice that stretches forever until it melds with the frozen blue of the sky or the faraway rise of tumbled snow and stone that is King William Island. The island caught, itself, by a hard sea.

And still. When it is still, I stand here on the *Terror*'s deck until my eyes ache and stream from the white that shines everywhere but on this black hulk and that of the *Erebus* wedged close by … and I think. I remember, as in a story told once, an unlikely story about friends and loves. A story so estranged from the reality of this bearded sea captain wrapped in frosted wool and oiled skin that it does seem to me it never happened at all.

Lord Franklin was my friend and we, I am certain I recall, travelled the seas for its secrets, adventured where the waves were high and black and the wind whipped full of the crackling splinters of ice. He is dead, I know as if told by an acquaintance of an acquaintance. Though he had spent so many months at his well-inked, well-scratched desk planning to stave off the cold in these ships of ours. Lamplit nights running his sharpened

61

pencils along the ruler to demonstrate where piped hot water should flow. Yet he was still no match for this careless North. Though we are reinforced with great iron planks and had mighty steam – great, thrashing demon-horses like wild phantoms – to drive our propellers, and we have food sealed in tins to last years. This is a merciless, loveless place; the steam but phantasms after all, and sucked away to nothing.

I can hear my own breathing. The cold tears at my lungs. And yet I have no heart to go below, where the sick lie in their bunks and die of blood spoiled by black frostbite, spit up their lungs while others wait their turn, quiet in the stench of sickness and sadness. They have emptied eyes, pouched in gray skin drawn loose over bones. Many have their wrists and ankles bound because these have weakened; my men buckle like marionettes. Their words drift away with their thoughts.

We taste our own rot.

And I am one too, who binds ankles and wrists, and must support one hand with the other when I eat, and shake my head trying to recall names and faces, places and old, old friends. I write to catch my thoughts before they escape, but the pencil falls from my fingers. Pain rips through me; I understand the screams of my men at night.

But I know, because I wrote it then, while I could, that Lord Franklin died on June 11th, 1847, when his heart faltered and stopped. We have lived a winter's night here since. We had lived here a winter's night before then. Months, where a day's light was a mere, brief glimmer between dark dawn and dark dusk. Twice, there has been no spring thaw.

Sometimes the air itself jibbers around me; the white glows. We are enclosed as in a pearl. A day swings by like a minute while I grasp at a thought. A man takes a year to open his tin, ripping at the corroded solder with the opener's hook, pours the mess onto a plate, to share, though nobody has the stomach for it and everyone simply stares. The body of the ship shudders as the ice squeezes.

Remember, remember the flags waving and the cheers as we set forth once more, glorying again in the adventure to the North, the sight of walls of ice, diamond-blue, and the play of eerie lights – God's fingers dancing in the skies – proud at the urging of Britain and our Queen to find the Passage for our sailors and the Empire's trade. The top-hatted speechmakers in parks and in Parliament; columns of pontifical prose in the newspapers. The moustachioed bandleader wooden on his dais, flicking his baton; the *oompah-oompah* off-key as somehow bands always must. Well-bred young men queuing to sign their names: second sons in silks and white smiles set to venture among the whales for history.

The celebrations for our forthcoming discoveries were much the same in Lord Franklin's Hobart Town as they were in my own, Irish Banbridge, though it was there in green Ireland I found my young lady to hang on my arm. Miss Sophia, her ladyship's niece, whose face wavers here before me, without form, though I know who it is hovering just beyond my sorry, icicled bridge, white ribands and lace streaming away from her bonnet and her pure-white neck towards the horizon. I have her letters in my trunk below. Had she agreed to marry me, would she have striven, as my friend Ross's wife strove, to keep him from the sea, and would I have stayed, and would I be warm now, by a fire, with my dogs and my children and my pipe? She laughed, said I was already married, and it is a wretched pain now to think my hand had indeed always grasped this tiller, to this end, and to think she might have accepted me had I been more gallant than sincere.

Green Ireland. The stony bridge that stretches its stocky, mossy arm across the Cut. Autumn leaves shaken from high elms onto the High Street. Smoke from stolid chimneys.

When James Ross was with me, long ago, we stood on our decks, I on my *Terror* and Ross on his *Erebus*, and watched the looming from the sea of an ice mountain that spat fire and smoke to the skies. There was a grumble that rolled to us across the chilled, chopped waters and shook itself into our fingers as we gripped the railing. We named this angry tyrant *Mt Erebus*. Perhaps it still smokes, fire rolling down its sheer sides with the hiss of flame meeting ice. I told this story many times to dinner parties where ladies' diamonds winked feebly in candlelight, with brilliantined men silenced and my Lord Franklin intent at the head of his table, wine in his hand, nodding and pink-cheeked.

To the east of *Mt Erebus* is the smaller, extinct volcano which we named *Mt Terror*, and at its foot is the cape named for me, and another cape nearby now *Cape Downshire* for my friend the Marquis, and all reached through the *Ross Sea*. A world away, a pole away. Our names are written with the finest of nibs on a map drawn in ice-white and blue.

Mere names, of men too small to escape.

The corners of my eyes are crisp with ice.

We have left many graves on this voyage, hewn into the frozen rock by unhappy men heaving for breath. Each man could chip at the rock and gravel only briefly with the pickaxe, before his fellow must take over while the first trembled and retched.

Sometimes, now, I sit at my desk and stare at the litany of names. Names, more names – a list of men whom I cannot recall through the fog that so circles my mind – and I read how we fashioned graves for them when they died, and wrote a short epitaph on their stones, and sang. The first of these died, oh, a century ago, seems a thousand years since, on land, before we sailed to our fate here to be caught fast in this vast, slow grip which is our world, our universe that was and is, and shall be, on and on and forever.

The days are longer. More time for madness: from boredom, from listlessness, from hunger. On my ascent to the bridge I stop, one leg up and one leg down, and listen and clench my sad teeth to remember why it was I climbed and then why it was I stopped. Remember that there was the sound of a scuffle but now there is only a scratching, the reason for the aggravation gone like a wisp just as I had forgotten hearing it. I pull myself to the bridge, to stand and stare. I stare each day for as long as I can, screwing my old eyes to peer between the folds of frosted scarf wound about my face, across the ice toward King William Island.

I descend to the fug below, since I have stood so long on my bridge on shaking legs that night has nearly come and I am driven to descend. To the febrile whisperings, wet hacking, the creak of a man crouching toward a bucket. In my cabin I close the log in which I have recorded all of our loss. The map, another blue map, hangs pinned to the wall, and a pin stands in the map to mark where we are held fast.

I am left all alone to captain these two ships that cannot sail, these one hundred-and-some men who cannot shanty for sadness.

I am sick of nothingness, sick of hopelessness heaped upon my back, sick of striving for decision when all thought is marsh. I shuffle paper covered with dancing scratchings. A page falls from my desk.

On deck I walk the length of my ship to hear my footsteps sound on the timber. The men chip away the ice from ropes and iron and balustrade; I have sent some to chip ice for water. I patrol my deck, back and forth. Back and forth. The sky is blinding, cold-blue. Clouds gather and scud; the world is full of racing gray-white, gray-white shadow and I stop to grip the railing to stop my dizzy falling. The sound of voices drops like pebbles, then whips away. I stand with care, stamp loudly and turn slowly, mindful of my ankles. Men move by inches, tired men both here, near to me where I can hear the struggle of their breathing, and yonder on the *Erebus,* where small figures creep at their work. We must have clean water: I call out, though I must stop to think. Men pause on their careful way. Patient as any empty vessel, they raise their eyes and wait. I order a party to chip ice.

I turn my head to the island and I am amazed. So close, so very close. I hold out my hand. Why, I could hold this island in my palm! This untidy heap, smudge of snow and gravel. All these months, and I could hold it in my palm!

I order a party to chip ice.

Our days are still brief. Below, in the long night, we listen to the banshees of the wind, crazed keening from horizon to horizon, the universe gone choleric, vicious, the ropes humming until the ice coats them again. Men whose faces are bone and whose lips are gray wrap their arms around themselves and rock. Many men are rocking. There is a high note held by someone, twin to the wailing that fills existence outside our ship.

I tap incessantly. I tap with my empty pipe; my mind buzzes with an excitement which I cannot fathom but carries me through the shrieking night.

Snow has blown up against our ships. Each ship has a snow-mantle, and shards of ice strike at angles, in the direction of last night's wind. The sky is polished clean of cloud, and there lies the island, a step away. And beyond that there is a company post at Hudson Bay where men of will could travel, surely, over land and over the iced sea. A step, two steps.

We have cut loose the frozen ropes that held one of our boats and the boat lies on the ice. I remember I thought last night: we must have a boat. I may have thought; I might remember it. Perhaps, if I did, I thought we may come across a thaw somewhere, perhaps I did. In any case, we have cut it loose and the men hobble about, smiles stretched across their faces like rips in canvas, glad of an order, glad of movement. Some weep, a weak escape of air hissing as they work. Slow work, slow work, and then men stand bent over, arms about each other's necks and quivering.

We must fill our boat, now, take the precious with us, wrack our remembrances for what is precious and think what one needs when one reaches the world. When we reach cabins and warm fires we will sing and thank the Lord Almighty, and so we must carry our books of prayer, I say, and five sailors fetch these in their bandaged arms. My thoughts fly here and there; fragments flick out of sight and back. I breathe deeply and stand tall, though then I am suddenly dizzy and must reach for support. Save what can be saved of value, of course, and sailors fetch for me the silverware that sits locked in the galley and the captains' quarters, with a shirring pile of plates, for we are civilised folk and will eat from them when we are well enough in the world to eat once more. I pick up one elegant serving spoon, which glints, and I turn it to see my initials scratched there, and turn it again to see my family crest at the base of its handle. I am grown short of breath; the sailors who stand around me pant also, waiting for an utterance. This is ... auspicious, and must be done right. My desk, I whisper, is of value to the world, and when we find the world there will be need to tell our story on it. My voice unsteady, I discuss with a sailor, whose mouth is full of blackened gum with three brown, wobbling teeth, how we could fetch Lord Franklin's desk also, for it was my friend's and has seen so much for so long. But it will not fit. My thoughts are black with this impossibility and, for sad minutes, I cannot speak for grief. The sailor puts his hand on my shoulder. We wait while sailors struggle slowly, pause and pant, with my desk wrapped in ropes and jerking downwards to the floor of ice by pulley. Where is the silver? More, there is room for a little more. All are hurrying slowly, each breath a dragging pain, but every sunken eye bright. A voice suggests curtain rods, and I am puzzled, then I agree that they are beautifully wrought, and the world will remember and approve that we thought to save them and also, it occurs, they could provide a fire if we were so minded and needed it. Yes, indeed.

Sailors wrap our laden boat with rope; their fingers bleed through ragged gloves and they slip and stumble, yet still they attempt a breathless, whispery, working song. And we set off, dragging the boat, towards the island that sits in the palm of my hand.

We will walk across the frozen sea.

Titian's Rose

Clare Girvan

Ave Maria, gratia plena.

This is a cold chapel despite my furs, but here I must stay on my creaking knees, until the maundering dotard in the pulpit gives us permission to rise. Which is not much of an improvement - the benches are hard, with backs as straight as Heaven's gate, and nowhere to put my legs for ease. I bundle my robes up behind me for what comfort I can get, but religion is no sport for a man of my years. And I am frankly bored by the flutters and whispers that go on around me - the rush of sibilants as the celebrated maestro Tiziano Vecellio takes his place.

Even the women are no consolation. What has become of the congregations of tender girls, so demure by their iron-faced duennas? I remember how Aretino and I would nudge each other as one of them let her eyes first slide slyly over the Communion cup, then close ecstatically as she thrust out her little red tongue to receive Christ's body! Little pleasure to be had nowadays from the sight of an ancient housewife's toothless mouth gaping at the priest's hand and dribbling down the side of the chalice.

Aretino used the church shamelessly as his bordello.

`Why, man,' he would say. `Where else will you find such an irresistible combination of sin and sanctity? To see a little virgin trying to keep her thoughts on Heaven once I have determined to have her - it's worth all the Rialto's best whores put together.'

Here they come, the dreary wine and wafers (supper, they call it) presented on a little white cloth, while my belly rumbles. My mind should be on the body and blood of our Lord, not the guinea fowls slowly basting in the kitchens back at Birri Grande. Nor the good bottles of Portuguese wine sent to me by King Philip himself to take away the taste of these slops.

Aretino despised the Eucharist and didn't care who knew it.

`If I want bread and wine,' he said once, his feet on the table as we toasted a new beauty marked down after Vespers, `I'll have it from my own kitchen and my own cellar, and save my digestion a deal of trouble. Give me a cask of Annibale's old Burgundy and I'll praise God with as much fervour as your canting priest in a year of Sundays.'

Pietro Aretino, Tuscan, Venetian, writer, pornographer, poet, dramatist, womaniser, blackmailer and flatterer, libel-monger and man of letters, as unscrupulous as a stoat; my dearest friend. Those who had crossed him and lived to regret it even called him dangerous, but we were like brothers for thirty years. He introduced me to everyone of consequence and there was hardly a palazzo in Venice that was not proud to have a portrait by Tiziano Vecellio hanging in one of its apartments.

The nobility befriended him eagerly - it was wiser than being his enemy - but nobody recognised a toady better than he did.

`Old so-and-so sent me a brace of pheasants yesterday,' he would say. `As a token of our friendship. Maybe he should ask his wife and daughter if they are also good friends to me.' And he would fling himself back in his chair and bellow with laughter until the bottle fell and smashed on the flagstones and his cringing dog fled shivering into a corner.

Life to him was as an antelope to a lion, to be shaken by the throat until it gave in. He was as coarse as a boatman and wore his clothes till they stank, but bragged that he could have a woman on her back within thirty minutes of making her acquaintance. In this, as so much else, he was not strictly truthful.

I miss him still. No one enjoyed a joke, a drink or a woman as he did. And I trusted him. Trust is itself untrustworthy; you can't rely on it. Oh, those cursed pictures. He kept his secret for over twenty years and almost went to his grave with it. But for his carelessness, I would never have known about it.

There are ghosts in this chapel. This was where she sat the day I first saw her; Violante, whose corn-coloured hair caught my eye in a rainbow cast

70

by this very same rose window that now lets in such a devil of a draught. Now there was a Venus, a Madonna, a saint or a sinner, anything else you care to name, by turns or all at the same time.

I was well on in years, with a wife in her grave and our children grown. I intended conquest and dalliance and nothing more. I never bargained for love.

She sat so still, her face raised to the holy cross, her breast heaving with her devotions till I feared (hoped, rather) that the dangerously-taxed bodice would no longer contain it. Never once in her prayers did her eyes waver from the suffering of Christ's blood-spattered form, but her little hand would steal about, to tweak a curl, stroke a shoulder, slide under a braided edge to scratch discreetly at a bite, smooth her skirts over her knees. And all done with such an air of innocent abstraction, as if to disclaim any accountability for the effect it was having on me. I set about her at once, naturally, my foil at the ready. Aretino was an acknowledged rapier-master, but I was no mean performer myself. So, en garde! Prima, the salute. First by sly peeps during the singing; the slow turn of the head, the glance, caught, instantly repealed, oh, an accident, I assure you. No offence, Madam. No response, either.

First thrust - a fumbled hymn book during the sermon; it crashed to the tiles, fluttering like a wounded pigeon as the priest drew breath for a tirade. The eye of her stern papa was upon me as I stooped to retrieve it, but I seized the opportunity of being down on my knees to favour her with a long, feverish look. She, blushing like a rose touched by sunlight, parried with a raised prayer book.

Secunda - a lunge; I dropped a glove - oh, your pardon, lady - and once more to my knees, close enough to see the rim of mud that edged the hem of her dress. Deo gratias, a hit! For in the space of a blink, her little stockinged foot popped out, riposted by pressing my hand gently to the floor, and retreated. She had taken off her shoes to be comfortable before God, bless her heart.

The last notes of music had scarcely reached the belfry before I was out of my seat and into the churchyard, leaning upon a cross like one of my old master's martyrs. As she came out she looked round as if puzzling where I had gone, but on seeing me, there came again that glorious, rose-

71

coloured blush and modest eyes. Papa and Mama were busy with the priest. There was no time to lose.

I bowed (no one performed the courtly bow as well as I did), sweeping the grass with my hat-feather.

`I hope I did not disturb your prayers too much, Madonna,' I said as she was about to pass me, dipping the edge of her hat to conceal her face. `I can't think what made me so clumsy.'

`I'm sure you will be forgiven, Maestro Vecellio,' she replied in a voice as soft and sweet as milk, pure as the heart of Our Lady. Then, like a shock of lightning through me, the lightest touch of her gloved hand on my arm, a little pinch with thumb and forefinger. From Madonna to minx in a moment. Well, I told you so.

One thing led to another - introduction to Ma and Pa de Palma (who were tickled to death by my magnanimity in speaking to them just like anyone else) followed by invitations to visit my studio.

The de Palmas arrived in famiglia, with a few chattering siblings in tow, all eager to court me and boast of it afterwards. The worthy parents were so delighted by my work and my humility that when I eventually put the suggestion (with such delicacy) that I would deem it the greatest honour if, there being no objection on their part, they would allow their daughter to sit for me one day. I assured them that Madonna Violante would be fully chaperoned, naturally.

`But Maestro Vecellio,' the mother gushed, clasping her hands fervently, `the honour would be entirely ours. And of course our daughter's. I'm sure Violante realises that.' (Violante was leaning out of the window, singing to herself and presenting me with a view of her swaying behind that made it difficult to keep my mind on the matter in hand.) `And as to propriety,' she went on, `I'm sure that no one would think wrong of a man of your stature.' She positively simpered.

`You're very kind,' I replied modestly. `I shall leave that question to you, then.' A master stroke; she would never send a chaperone now. `Shall we say ten o'clock tomorrow morning?'

She took to it like a salamander to the fire. (I mean, of course, the modelling. For all her maidenly blushes and fol de rols, maiden she was not; widow, in fact, the youthful relict of a petty official, and well practised in the amatory arts.) As a model she was unsurpassed. My skills were scarcely sufficient to cope with the astonishing luminosity of her skin, and even now, I am still not sure I got it right. Sometimes I would work a whole morning on the fall of light on a breast, then scrub it out again in the afternoon. She could hold a pose for an hour at a time, then recollect herself as prettily as if she had merely been asleep. She could be divine or wanton, joyous or sorrowful, pensive or passionate; she stood, sat or lay with the same voluptuous ease, never less than superb.

She became my mistress from that first morning visit, when she arrived dressed to kill in her Mama's idea of a suitable outfit - a full-skirted deep rose pink dress and bejewelled hat - and asked somewhat nervously what I required her to do.

I had been up half the night already in a fever of apprehension, stacking frames and canvasses out of the way, tidying my bench, dusting off the furniture, laying cushions on the dais, making sure of an adequate supply of wine, scheming for a seduction. But in the end, I couldn't get up the nerve, and who made the first move, after all? Why, she did, the sweet Magdalene.

For a full hour I stood her, sat her, moved her to light and shade, draped and contemplated her.

`Like this?'

`Perfect. Now turn a little more to the right - '

`Shall I stand here?'

`You're not too tired?'

`Not at all, Maestro.'

I had hardly dared to touch her; she it was who arranged folds and unlaced the front of her dress, just the tiniest bit, oh so decorously, and all in the interest of Art; hitched up her skirt to fiddle with a shoe, bent over to show a little more bosom. She was as artful as a monkey and ripe as a Vicenza pear, and in her dark pink dress she was Rosa Mundi, the matchless rose. I was lost from that hour.

`Shall I lie down?' And there she was, lying back on the couch, her arm languorously raised behind her head, her other hand resting below her stomach, fingers tucked into a fold. She was Venus, Lilith, - my breath and

73

my metaphors deserted me simultaneously. And how the devil had she managed to undo her bodice altogether without my seeing her do it?

It was like dying among roses to love her; a fell of hair, bright as pollen; leaf-green eyes, lit almost gold when the sun caught them; coral-red lips; blossom-white shoulders; pearly, pink-budded breasts with rose madder ridges beneath where her dress had pinched her; pale, sumptuous belly, the colour of honey mixed with cream, and the golden arrow below; soft, full-fleshed thighs that fell apart like petals tickled by a lusty bee, and the juicy, midnight-red nectar-place between.

She felled me like a thunderbolt from Jove himself. I drowned in love; I saw and felt only her. She invaded my dreams, her taste was in my mouth, her scent in my nostrils, and her very body so much a part of mine that sometimes I could scarcely distinguish between the two.

'Dio, man,' Aretino exclaimed. 'You are a schoolboy, forever mooning over her. I give it six months.'

I smiled and said nothing. He was outrageously frank about his own inammoratas, whom I pitied, for he showed no tenderness for them. I never knew if he fully understood the strength of my feelings for her. It strikes me now that there was much that we kept from each other. I believed then that we were a perfectly balanced triangle; that we had a rare intimacy which enabled her to appear naked before us both without affectation; that his friendship for me encompassed her impartially. Perhaps I made too little of what she was to me; perhaps I should have been more open with him. For fear of his mockery, I kept my feelings to myself. I think now that I may have made a great mistake.

He named her La Gloriosa, and he called round very often when she was working for me. She was never in the least put out by his knock on the door, but greeted him with lazy courtesy, scarcely disturbed enough to break off her singing. She sang constantly, without melody, like an untuned violin. I had a small caged bird hanging in the window, that struck up the moment the shutters were opened, and she liked to sing with it.

'Listen, Tizzi,' she would call in delight. 'He's trying to copy me. I'm sure he understands me.' And she would chirrup gaily at it, while it hopped, monotonously tweeting, off its perch and back again.

'By Our Lady,' Aretino remarked once, his finger in his ear, 'I am her slave, but she'd drive a man to distraction with her perpetual warbling.'

`I don't mind it,' I said, wiping a brush on a scrap of rag. `It's a pleasant accompaniment. I have no ear for music, anyway.'

`Fortunately for you, my friend.'

He was a strict critic, however, and even had the nerve to move her position occasionally `to improve the light, my dear fellow.' No one else would have dared to be so rash.

It does a man no credit to say that he produced his finest work under the influence of one bottle too many of strong Ligurian wine. It was my regard for his judgement, and the clouding of my own, that led me into one of the few acts of my life that I now regret. He talked me into it; he could have talked a Sister of Mercy into a brothel if the mood took him, damn the fellow.

`But think of it, Maestro,' he would say, using the name that others spoke with more respect. `So much beauty going to waste. Why should others be denied what you keep to yourself? It's merely selfishness, after all.'

`I'm a painter, not a gutter-artist,' I answered.

`You're going to tell me you have too much regard for her,' he said. `Or are you thinking of your reputation?'

`Well, there is that, but yes, I do have a regard for her, obviously.'

`Wouldn't she be willing?'

I smiled at that. `She probably would.'

`Well, then, where's the harm? Most other painters do the same. Pordenone has a collection of engravings that would make your hair curl.'

`If the word got out, I should lose half my patronage. Who would send their wives to me for a portrait after that? The little dyer is snapping at my heels already and seems to be quite well thought of. I don't see the point of jeopardising my position in society.'

`Speaking as a peddler of filth myself, old chap, I wouldn't say it's exactly done my own position much harm. In fact, I think it's done it good. Ladies in particular seem to find my stories most interesting.' He waggled his hand suggestively.

`That's different. You trade on it and glory in it. I have a respectable clientele.'

`Ha! Respectable! I could tell you a thing or two.'

`I'm sure you could. You'll end up at the bottom of the lagoon one of these days with your head in a sack.'

But he got round me at last, one warm night on the balcony at Birri Grande. Dinner was over: a dish of local eels, a couple of dozen eggs, a fine turkey cock with fennel, a quince jelly, figs and a pretty sugar pastry prepared by Violante herself under the careful eye of my sister Orosola. Dio, I can still taste those figs, a gift from Alessandro Farnese. The Farnese grew the best figs in the whole of the province, I swear.

I had lamps lit and the air was spiced with the scent of jasmine and lilies. Aretino sat on the wall overlooking Murano, eating apricots and spitting the stones into the flower vases. Little barques bobbed their prow lanterns on the dark water below, and a last hopeful mandolinist still sang to his lady. Half of the guests had gone home, but Bianca and Leonardo Molin were still canoodling and exchanging mouthfuls of wine by the fountain (they persisted in behaving like newly-weds in company, although their private rows were common knowledge). Violante and Caterina Sandella were inventing a mildly lascivious dance to a villanelle from the musicians, Sansovino was holding forth on the nature of learning and making a very dull job of it, Orosola had gone to bed, and Bembo was asleep.

`And so I postulate - ' droned Sansovino, `that if, as Plautus has it - '

Ping! Another shot at the urn. A flower head dropped. Aretino yawned.

`My dear old soul.' At his most languidly polite. `If I may ex-postulate, there are two extremely delightful ladies doing their very best to attract our attention, and I think it the greatest discourtesy to ignore them any longer. Maestro, are you coming with me, or must I attend to both myself?'

Violante suddenly executed a tipsy skip that tumbled both herself and Caterina to the flagstones in a fluster of skirts, bare legs and squeals of laughter. There was not much of the Madonna about her that night.

At twenty-five, she was magnificent, at the height of her ripeness. She had borne three children (one dead in infancy, alas) and it had left no mark upon her. Candlelight illuminated the bloom of her, cast shadows into her softnesses. I knew and adored every inch of her, and yet each time she appeared mysterious, changeable as the moon. It was a gift she had.

And so I drew her, while Aretino and Caterina plunged and groaned in the next room. I drew with a lashing, savage intensity, led on by the wine I had consumed. Like the good model she was, she knew my every thought, writhing lazily, turning and twisting herself while my pen scrabbled at the paper almost of its own accord. I grabbed fresh paper, more ink, a new pen, and still she metamorphosed before me in a thousand capricious, shameless forms. On and on I went, committing to the eager page every gleaming crevice, before I finally fell upon her and glutted myself like a starving wolf.

They were fine drawings. I looked at them by daylight with shame, but they were, admittedly, excellent.

`They're very good,' said Aretino critically, chewing at a hunk of bread. `I could get you a good price for them.'

`Let me see.' Violante was sitting up in bed, picking at a peach. She reached out a sticky hand and giggled. `Oh, dear. Oh, Tizzi, you're not going to show them to anyone? I'm sure I should die of embarrassment.'

`We should have thought of that yesterday,' I said. `I'll burn them.'

`My dear man, what's the problem? You've painted erotic subjects before. What about that Bacchanal for D'Este? Everyone knows what was going on there.'

`Only by implication. They were classical subjects. It was all most discreet.'

`Just an excuse for painting a lot of naked people. You painters fool yourselves and your public too. At least be honest and admit it.'

`Try telling that to my patrons.'

They would not be destroyed. They lay hidden under a damask in an old Spanish chest at the end of my studio, and I wore the key around my neck. Many times I tried to set fire to them, but though I got the flame near enough to drip wax onto the corners, I could never bring myself to do it. They were her, you see. They seemed to reproach me each time I secretly took them out and spread them on the floor, lighted candle at the ready, and I couldn't harm them.

Violante had one as a memento, strictly on the condition that she never divulged the artist's name, a promise she rather surprisingly kept, but the rest I could neither keep nor get rid of. They lurked in the dark, unseen, but constantly clamouring for justice.

Aretino took them in the end.

'I'll keep your damned secret,' he said. 'I'll make sure they stay hidden and you can have the key. But, Santo Volto, it's a terrible waste. You'd better pray I don't fall on hard times.'

I kept mainly to religious subjects and portraits after that. I, and perhaps she also, had been somewhat shaken at what I was capable of. There were one or two more classical, chastely erotic commissions, but Messer Vecellio was a man of honour and never overstepped the bounds.

'Six months,' Aretino said once, but he was wrong. It surprises me too, but we were together, she and I, for fifteen more years, close as two halves of a walnut.

Age suited her. She pinned her hair up into starched muslin caps and became rounded and cosy - we slipped into comfort as easily as you might an old doublet - and her children lived with mine as siblings. We were far from poor, but she went daily to the market to bargain for poultry and melons; she supervised the servants and pounded bread-dough energetically amid vast clouds of flour; she learned to entertain princes. In short, she took the reins of my household as if born to it.

There were no more children. She wanted them; she wept in the night; she prayed to the stone-faced Virgin in the church, puddling the flagstones with tears; she gave her silver locket to a pedlar for a scrap of St Peter's thighbone; she wore her rosary well-nigh to a thread. By the time her womb ceased flowering, she was resigned to it.

'It's my punishment, Tizzi. I've been very sinful.'

'You're an angel,' I said sincerely. 'If you mean those pictures, well, that was my fault. God can blame me if He likes.' I had never quite been able to rid myself of the feeling that I had betrayed her. God didn't come into it.

She became my comfort, my strength and my joy. As my eyesight began to fail, she read to me by the hour, squinting in the candlelight. When we ran out of books, she wheedled more out of swindling old Balducci for half the price and a home-baked pigeon pie. She supervised my studio, hired my models (sternly chaperoned, always!) and was not slow to give her opinion of a painting. I was sometimes less than accurate, my fingers troubled by rheumatism, but how she made me work at it.

`You have a reputation, Tizzi. Your patrons expect the best of you. Now try again.' I grumbled, but obeyed.

Aretino was away during those years, soft-soaping the nobility in sundry provinces; we saw little of him. He wrote occasionally - sly, witty, libellous letters, concerning the hypocrisy of the Duke of A, or the adulteries of the Princess of B. Apparently, his book was doing particularly well in Ferrara, and was much admired by the Abbess of San Bernardino, natural daughter of the Borgia. Fame indeed.

But on the day of her death, he was at my door within four hours. He said not a word, but dropped from his horse and wrapped his great arms round me, his warm bear-smell as comforting as a sheath of fur. Through my grief, I was astonished to see tears in his eyes.

You want to know what happened to those drawings? I'll tell you. I burned them. Yes, I finally did, every one.

When Aretino also died, I went to his house. Everything was in an uproar, and hardly anyone noticed me among the mourners and avaricious relatives.

His body had been removed, and the bedchamber was empty. There was little worth squabbling over, save for a few oddments of furniture and the bed where his corpse had lain (a grey hair still question-marked on the pillow). His apartments downstairs were sumptuous, but a bedchamber to him was a place for two things only and he saw no point in embellishment. `I am either asleep or playing sword-in-the-scabbard,' he would say. `Why waste money on fancy nonsense, when nobody is looking at it?'

I took the drawings from the cupboard where he kept them, and was just putting them hastily into a canvas bag when I noticed a fold of paper underneath them. I opened it without much curiosity. It contained a small withered object, a pressed rose that broke into brown flakes even as I took it out. For a moment I puzzled over it; it was hardly Aretino's style, a sentimental pressed flower, such as might have been given him by ... a thought from nowhere, a speck, a mere seed; but it grew, a great beanstalk of a thought, that popped out huge ugly leaves and blotted out the light, until in no time at all I was searching madly, scrabbling in drawers, under the bed, hardly knowing what I was searching for.

It didn't take long. I found them; letters, in her girlish handwriting, mawkish with endearments. Letters to him, twenty, twenty five years old. I read them all. Handkerchief forgotten, I sat on the bed and snuffled and blubbered my way through every one, drenching them with a buffoon's tears. And then I took them home, along with the drawings, burned the lot in an old mixing bowl, and threw the ashes into the sea.

Dio, has the priest not yet done with his drivellings? My knees pain me and I want my dinner. I have no interest in his rantings over sins I am too old to commit. I come but to worship God and pay my way to Heaven, followed by a quick genuflection by the Carrara headstone that bears Aretino's name.

He is dead, and so is she; everyone is dead and only I am left; a sullen, old, old man surrounded by phantoms and the leftovers of a life.

For a while I howled in corners; I destroyed his books and her likeness and denied myself memories. For a while I lived crouching in shadows, devoted to a vengeful God and letting the dust accumulate. But Philip of Spain was pestering me for a Venus, my students were complaining, and eager young women arrived constantly on the doorstep with letters of introduction. So I began again.

I keep Aretino's shrivelled old rose in a small pewter box in my studio. It will accompany me to my grave, in memoriam, a little of both to take with me to heaven.

He always said he would outlive me; I don't think he ever thought I would find out. It was an act of true friendship to hide it so well. As for her, I believe she made amends for it; she loved me well enough. It was all so long ago; it looks different now, and I am too old to be less than grateful.

The little dyer finally achieved eminence, despite my efforts. Maestro Tintoretto he is these days, and a nice enough chap, I suppose. Strange, how little it matters. I can barely hold a brush in my twisted hands anyway, and sometimes paint with my fingers from sheer impatience. My pictures are half-completed by my students, and a rare bodge they make of them, but they sell like pieces of the true cross all the same. Maestro Vecellio is still a celebrity himself, and anything goes. They would buy his cast-off underlinen if it was offered.

And my reputation is impeccable.

At last ...

The priest gets to, `And finally, my brethren – '. I stand up cautiously. A touch of dizziness; it's nothing. Head, heart, shoulder, shoulder. Lord, raining again; more damp in the joints.

Nunc dimittis. God rest their souls.

Amen.

In the Valley of the Trinity

Sheila MacAvoy

We tramped into the town with broken shoes, the stage having collapsed into the river rocks five miles earlier, just below Douglas City. The horses had been unhitched from the stage and the goods belonging to the men from Sacramento were unloaded from the innards of the creaking carriage (along with the human cargo of Sunny and me) and then lashed to sledges fashioned from lodge pole pines. The rest of us, me and Sunny and the six miners, carried what we could of our own things. I had a dog house bag made of some unfortunate beast's hide that had been tanned to an improbable, but eye catching, eagle's beak yellow. Sunny had only a satchel that was once a paisley shawl. The magenta and carmine tracings were travel-blurred into a uniform gray.

From the stage landing at Redding we had traversed the Eastern side of the Trinity Mountains and rattled over its parched brown earth as the track twisted through sandstone-lined canyons. The place was dry as a handkerchief at a whore's funeral. It took three days just to get over Buckhorn Summit, the shaking and rattling eventually taking its measure of our ship of fools. When we descended the western flank of the range and gazed into the dark green interior, we entered another country entirely. Once under the canopy of trees, the sounds of the stage wheels were softened by the enclosing embrace of greenery and we saw the work of miracles that centuries of rains had done. The great trees rose in silent glory and were said to be too immense for five men to circle their girth. And in the granite creases above our heads, the roar of water, even in the summer's heat, filled our ears.

In their excitement, the men began to push ahead, urging the animals with whips and, as the horses strained to avoid the lash, tin pans and tools and rolls of screen tumbled to the side of the way and bounced off the stones embedded in the beaten track.

Sunny stopped to retrieve a pan, a wide flat tilted pan, fashioned from tin and soldered at its seams by a competent tinker; it was shaped for the easy placer gold that lay in the shallow streams.

'This will do for my biscuit,' she said and tucked it in her paisley bundle.

'Best not let those fellows see you. They look to be hard ones,' I said.

'They are too busy running their way to paradise.' She laughed when she said that, a laugh that raised her chin and displayed her smooth long neck.

Sunny and I had become acquainted on our voyage out from the Lower Bay in New York Harbor where we found ourselves leaning over a rail to watch the Buttermilk Channel pass under our keel.

'Farewell to thee, stern master,' I said, throwing a thumb in the direction of the wharves and counting houses stacked up against the Battery.

'And farewell to tubs and scrub boards,' answered Sunny in her country woman's slur.

'No earning bread upon our knees.'

'Well, now,' said Sunny. 'I wouldn't go so broad as that.'

We had both laughed and moved closer so we could hear over the clatter of the ship, over the shouts and grunts of the sailors mixed with the horns and whistles of the crowded Bay. When Sandy Hook passed by in the morning haze, we chose to go below to be out of the way.

'Shall we repair to our cabin, Madam?' I said, linking my arm in hers. We made our way into the hold and settled into a corner forward of the steering post, stretching out on our shawls and curling up back to back. There were no bunks in that part of the hold, but, from our perch in the corner, none of the other passengers could steal our goods or surprise us.

When our three-masted packet cleared the Port of New York, bound for Chagres in the Panamas, the Master Pilot offloaded to a skiff propelled by an oarsman with the most amazing chest muscles recently seen by either of us. We were to see more of the masculine form on our pack train across the Isthmus of Panama to the Pacific port on the other side of that God forsaken, vermin infested, unforgiving piece of ground. There, the men had been neat and lean and brown as butternut.

It was full summer when we pushed into the camp at the place called Weaverville. Ahead of us women, a hundred yards ahead the miners trotted with purpose, whooping and laughing like nervous boys. The last horse in the train dragged grinders, wheels, shovels and rocker parts used to pound or shake the yellow metal out of its stony prison. There was, also, a small cast-iron stove. Foam streamed from the animal's mouth and, at last, the horse stopped and swayed and fell first to its knees and then, with a groan, flopped over on its flank. His sides heaved deep and he made whistling sighs.

'What can we do for this poor creature?' I said. It seemed so hard, just walking past the dumb beast who had served so well.

'Do? We can do ourselves the honor of moving on.'

'But Sunny. It might only take a bit of water.'

She looked at me with her large eyes and smiled with her cheerful grin. 'You are a softy, so. Nothing can help that poor beast, except lots of tending, and we don't have time for that.'

We went on and I stumbled over a stone, falling to my knee and skinning my last pair of cotton stockings. Try as I might, I could not keep away the thought of the animal dying behind us, the sight in my mind's eye of the men wrenching the goods off the sledge. Sunny patted my arm as if I were a child of two.

'You are a soft one, my pet. There will be little mercy for us ahead.'

This place was named for the miner, Sebastian Weaver, who got here among the first. A fast-moving creek came down from the foothills and flew by the town to join the Trinity River. We passed the spot where two branches of Weaver Creek parted and cut a deep gorge in the rock, spinning fast down a sharp descent, dumping into a wider pool. Beyond that place, the creek made a bend, and a bar of gravel had built out from the banks. In the bar, we could see the men, miners all, on their knees, patiently washing the gravel in their wide pans. We made our way along the steep track into the town.

'A girl could break a leg here,' I said.

'Break a lot more than that,' said Sunny.

It was spread out in front of us, a basin of trampled earth, wooden buildings lined up beside a dusty road that took a wicked turn as it left the town, ruts and rocks, pigs rooting in the ruts. At the madcap bend in the road, a mammoth tent balanced on poles and gleamed white against the deep blue mountains in the distance. We were to learn that the tent sheltered a gambling casino that had been in continuous operation since the first dust was shaken out of the streams. One of the roadside buildings had a circular stairway made of iron tracery, foreign fancy work that reminded me of some Paris balconies and recalled the salad days of my early youth. It must have shipped from San Francisco. This giddy decoration curled upwards to a shaded veranda that contained a sprawled chair and a brilliant parrot in a rusty cage.

'Look beyond,' Sunny said.

Curved around the town, blue and soft in the summer heat, the stand of mountains rose like a stage set, snow still dusting the top peaks even though it was already July.

'Those are big beauties,' I said.

'I hear it told they are the Trinities.'

We came to the building with the circular stairs and entered on the first level. Inside, barrels, kegs, sacks and tin boxes leaned against each other, bursting with seed, flour, tallow and beans. Leather, chain, butchered chickens, rope, ears of dried corn, and lanterns in many shapes hung from the rafters.

'Mr. Charlie B. Hampton?' Sunny asked.

'Up the stairs, Ma'am.'

By suppertime, we were in a small room at the back, a room with one bed, no window, and a slop jar painted with a yellow and black butterfly on its side. Wasn't even a chair to rest in. Sunny took the bed and I took the floor, using her shawl satchel for a pillow, and soon we were both sleeping the sleep of the just.

There were two kinds here; those that mined for the yellow metal, those that fed off the miners' needs - for food, shelter, and equipment, not to mention whiskey and whores - and those that played with both. In short supply was gold and women. Charlie B. Hampton was of the second kind, a purveyor of general merchandise. But he had dreamed bigger and he sent for Sunny Hurley and me to open a boarding house that would be not much use for boarding. To gain her agreement, he had signed over a Note to her on the goods in his store. What she didn't know was the Note had been sold more than once.

For the first weeks we were ridden hard, although the single bed required that we alternate between Sunny and me. Sunny was not one for two whores in the same bed, a finer point that made me wonder if she was really as thick-skinned as she seemed. She also found a better use for the tin pan salvaged on the track. She used it to lather and wash the privates of every man who paid his way between her legs.

'Another quarter ounce,' Charlie used to say as the dirty water flew off the veranda into the rutted street below. He kept good track of the payments in gold dust in this way. At the end of a month, we had enough dust to buy a second bed.

But Sunny had other ideas.

'Mister Charlie,' she said. I evaluate we need to expand on this premises before the church women get to town.'

'You evaluate, do ye?'

'Yes, Mister Charlie.' She looked straight into his face with her wide-set hazel eyes. Sunny Hurley was not what you would call pretty, her nose was too long for that, but she knew how to hold her chin high so she could look down it in a mysterious way. It always got a man fidgeting for his bank notes or his dust.

All her evaluating only got her permission from Hampton to erect the expansion of the premises herself. Since he already owed her either the price of the goods in the store or the goods themselves, she didn't worry much about who would own the expanded building. In her mind she figured she'd own it all.

At Big Bar, two miles and a bit along the track that followed to the course of the Trinity, a sawyer worked wood into boards. His mill straddled a section of the torrent that had been driven aside by the mine tailings, creating a reliable mill race. Sunny soon had enough gold dust to buy the cut lumber that would make up the extension to Hampton's General Merchandise Emporium. By late fall, the wood was up, a two and a half story lean-to which added one room up and three down. There was a small scullery too. Sunny was a caution for clean towels and drawers.

The winter came to the basin early that year and along with the change in the weather came Alexander Lockhart.

'That feller is sure a lovely sight,' Sunny said the first time he clanked into Hampton's general store.

Alex was taller than most and, it turned out, meaner than most. He had a neat, well-trimmed moustache and he bathed without prodding. He wore buff color moleskin pants that advertised his finicky nature and a dark leather hat, high in the crown and soft in the brim, so much so that it was hard to read his face when the lid was clamped on his head with a firm hand. This day, though, he removed his hat to shake off the silver dollar sized snow flakes that were streaming from the sky in one of the early storms. His eyes were dark and deep, like agate stones, fringed with thick lashes that veiled whatever thoughts galloped across his mind.

By nightfall, he was with Sunny in the upstairs room and her squealing and his banging could be heard below. Charlie sent up reinforcements in the form of a pair of bear steaks cooked pretty bloody and a bottle of brandy from his secret stash. The two didn't come out for three days and, when they did, they looked like they had been in a tussle, with Sunny's hair ever which way and Lockhart's moleskins rumpled like they had rolled in them together. As might be expected, Sunny broke all her own rules and got soft on one of the customers. It was brief, a few weeks at most; Sunny soon got her wits back and started entertaining her regular boys. But she had been bitten, poor lamb.

Snow on the roof of the upstairs rooms in the boarding house made the inside quiet and cozy. Fingers of ice decorated the eaves. By now, Sunny had four new girls working the lean-to extension, a Mexican from the Yucatan who refused to look her customers in the face when she serviced their requirements, a Chinese, who was favored by the boys from back East, I suppose because she was small and seeming shy, and two Irish ladies like Sunny and me who did whatever it took. For we Irish tarts, it was the lesson of the long trip from Queenstown to Sacramento.

We joked about the wear of the trade; Martecca from the Yucatan exaggerated the callous on her elbows and Min Ya giggled that her neck was stiff from feigning innocence. We Irish whores complained about the hard beds and the scarcity of vaporous liniments to ease our sore parts. But we all accepted the gold dust tribute and only skimmed a bit before we delivered a share to Sunny.

We all thought that Lockhart would suit up and move off and not take Sunny's resumption of the trade as a personal rebuke. He did leave for a while, after a few weeks sucking on his whiskey in a corner table at the White Star Saloon. None of us reckoned on the power of the male flame when it has been ignited by a certain whimsy. Nor on the lure of such a light for Sunny, our little Painted Lady.

Lockhart had prospected in all parts of the upper Trinity Valley and had dug and panned these past few years in one camp after the other, always striking early and clearing out after the easy pickings were exhausted. Those who mined the Feather River in Butte County remembered him as big, sullen and unsociable. He was from Missouri, it was said, and so he had knowledge of nothing but hard driving and bare ground.

That spring, Lockhart trotted back into town on his chestnut mare and took up residence in the rear of the new drug store operating next to Hampton's Emporium. It made a nice pair, the drug store and the dry goods, and Lockhart was in the thick of it, able to keep an eye on the trade and also on Sunny. He no longer went off to his diggings, but drifted through town, from the casino to the Chinese sporting house below the river to the new saloon on the upper road.

Within weeks of his return, he circulated a petition seeking election as the Sheriff of Trinity County. He had a few opponents, mostly newer arrivals who were intent upon cleaning up the place. Lockhart ran on a platform of faster claims, a planked road through camp, and incorporation of a local bank. Himself as the president, of course.

He was elected, although some said the votes were not honest, that he had paid hungry prospectors for ballots along the track back to Eureka where he was to deliver the official count. No matter. Alex Lockhart became the first Sheriff of Trinity County and, until a system of courts and civil juries were official, he would leave the administration of justice to the Miners' Courts.

No amount of suasion could keep Sunny from what she thought was her right. After some heady months of business in the lean-to boarding house, Sunny took the idea that it was time to make her claim for the store and goods for which she held the Promissory Note. We ladies were never to understand why she went in her mind toward respectability. Perhaps it was her fear of the church women who were coming, and of the changes they would demand. Perhaps it was the sight of Lockhart, all more than six feet of him, dark whiskered and sullen. Perhaps when he won for Sheriff, she feared that he would bring her down, one way or the other.

So, in late Spring, she made a demand on Hampton for the goods in the store, presenting her Note within earshot of several miners who were recuperating from a night in Sunny's back rooms with us women. Whence, Hampton confessed that he had already posted a bond, with the goods as surety, to men in San Francisco in exchange for the new inventory, which was expected overland from Eureka on the Coast. At which point, Sunny set up the claim that Hampton's store, with its present stock of goods, belonged to her; she demanded that a jury decide on the ownership.

'I will have my store and goods by right of a promise written,' she said.

'You would take your chance with Sheriff Lockhart?' I asked, the Sheriff having been elected on the previous fortnight.

'One Sheriff does not make a jury,' said Sunny, rather grandly with her chin higher than usual.

When Lockhart heard of her demand, he refused to even call a miners' jury on the ground that her claim was not the oldest. He said it was the Law in California that the oldest was the better right. Since when did California have a law to call its own? When the miners in the Hampton Store, whether from a sense of fairness or a sense of fun, heard of Lockhart's low refusal, they did what had long been justice in these camps. They called their own jury.

Luckily, it was bright and dry on the day the self-appointed town committee called the miners together in order to decide the ownership of the Hampton Emporium. There was such a crowd of men and boys in the forefront of Hampton's, they spilled into the road, pushing and craning to get a look at Sunny, dressed in modest black and switching a small dove feather fan back and forth across her handsome face. She sat up front, the only woman in a room full of men, most of whom had been her customers. I could see all these goings-on through the spy hole behind the dry goods counter.

Then the business began. Quiet fell over the room and Ned Frobischer, the Methodist preacher in town this day on his monthly circuit of the river camps, called the room to order. Being the only person around who could write with reliability, Ned had appointed himself the scribe. Fishing in his saddle pouch, he brought out a stick pen and a bottle of black ink.

'Nominations for judge will be entertained,' he said, his pen poised over a sheet of paste board. No miner challenged him and the work began. A judge, Clarence Perkins, keeper of the Albany Saloon, first oldest saloon in town, was selected by a show of hands and a jury of twelve miners, all working their diggings in the valley of the Trinity River, was agreed upon. Then they recessed for refreshment, exhausted by the excitement and by feelings of success, which to a miner, is the equal of a hundred-dollar nugget.

Several crocks of liquor appeared from under chairs and from behind barrels, and were quickly passed from man to man, with a polite wipe of the sleeve over the neck of the jug to signify the man had manners. Almost all lit a cheroot or a previously rolled tobacco cigarette. They had come to the meeting prepared.

Judge Perkins slammed his fist on the counter of the store and called the jury back to business, his beaver hat quivering with the importance of sudden dignity.

'We need to get this work done before midday as the Redding Stage arrives by noon.' Perkins paused and added, 'If it arrives,' at which remark, everyone, even Sunny, laughed. She was remembering our entrance into the camp some months passed, victims of busted springs.

From my spy hole beside the room, I could see what many could not. He must have silenced his dog leather boots with axle grease because, without a solitary sound, Sheriff Lockhart slipped into the rear of the store, just inside the doorway, and stood for a moment very still, filling the frame with his dark silhouette. Then he melted into the swarm of standees at the back, as much as a man half a head taller than the rest could disappear in a crowd. He, like all the others, kept his hat on, in spite of the lady present. In this circumstance, Sunny was regarded as a lady, being out of uniform, so to speak.

She stood and walked to the front, half turning so that the judge and jury could hear her speak. I sensed her flinch, a tensing of the body that few would notice, as her eye caught the dark shape of the man at the back, Sheriff Lockhart. It is a wonder of nature how two people who are drawn together can spot the shape of the other's body, the tilt of the head, the angle of the shoulders, the motion of the limbs from a distance of a quarter mile, it seems. In this confined space, Sunny could count his whiskers.

She presented the Note of Charlie Hampton to Judge Perkins and waited for his next word, her hands hanging relaxed and quiet by her sides. There was about her a mood of resignation as, I do believe, she thought the miners would cause her harm.

'Your Honor, Judge, this paper bears the truth. The property in Mr. Hampton's store is mine by right of fair bargain and contract and the shop itself is also. More, Your Honor, the extension back of the place was made with my own money and my own boards and is mine outright.' Her voice was clear, though soft with the accents of her home place at the far side of the world.

Judge Perkins took the Note from Sunny's hand and spread it flat before him, peering close at the markings. It was a slim folded page, bent many times to view, and I had a clear sense that our esteemed Judge could not read or cipher. He turned to Scribe Frobischer, who was busy at the counter end, scratching on his makeshift ledger. They whispered words, back and forth, directly into each other's ear. Whereupon, Frobischer read the paper again and nodded his head. Rather stingily, under the circumstances.

'This Note, in my opinion is genuine and lays out the contents of the stores in Hampton's place to be of the value as of 1851, month of October, day sixteen, at 4,000 US dollars gold or the whole lot, stores and caboodle, whichever makes up the dollar number.'

There were a few whistles from the crowd, joined in by the jury; one shoeless boy stood to his feet and did a little dance of approval. Judge

Perkins looked up from the Note in front of him and said nothing, but was stern and judgely.

'I call Mister Charlie B. Hampton to testify.'

From the rear, Mister Charlie shuffled forward on bandy legs, a small man with badly trimmed whiskers that hung in his morning's breakfast grease in two sad strings from the corners of his mouth.

'This your signing?'

'It is mine, Judge.'

'Was you sober?'

'As a judge, Judge.' A titter.

'Is there four thousand US gold in stores inside your place?'

'No, Your Honor. There is three thousand US gold in stores and one thousand US gold to the value of the built rig.'

'So, the whole lot is of the value four thousand?'

'That is true,' said Charlie B., God bless his eyes. I knew he'd figure a way to stay in Sunny's good grace in fair payment for all those slow, winter afternoons spent on his seedy couch.

'Take your place back, Hampton.'

Judge Perkins then handed the Note to the juryman seated first at the end.

'Please, look at this paper and say if it is genuine to you and pass this to your fellows.'

The jurymen gazed at the paper, those that could read with less intensity than those who pretended. Across one row and down the other, the paper travelled, hand to hand. Sunny followed it with her eyes and glanced up from time to time to see the tall Sheriff in the back scowling from under his high crowned hat.

'Missus Sunny, have you proof you built the lean-to?'

'I have no paper, Judge.'

From the back, the sawyer from Big Bar stepped forward.

'I sold the board, your Honor. Enough to make a lean-to.' He doffed his canvas cap and ducked his head of thinning hair in Sunny's direction. From some desperate afternoon of longing, all the way down the track from Big Bar, he, too, owed a debt to Sunny. She was not always fussy about services on credit, the sign of a rank amateur.

93

'Anyone see the raising up?'

About five hands waved, a few in the jury row, all without hesitation.

'Anyone work on the raising?'

Same five and a few more now. The case was building.

'Who paid?'

'Sunny,' they said at once, in unison. Then everyone coughed and moved in their seats and generally acted impatient. The judge saw no sense in going further.

'How does the jury vote? Raise hands for Sunny as owner.'

Twelve hands were raised.

'Case dismissed. Sunny owns the Hampton Emporium.'

It was notable even then that no alternative owner had been suggested. Thus, it was a surprise when Sheriff Lockhart stepped forward from the gray space in the rear of the store and spoke.

'Your Honor, there is a lien on this store and goods which has been sent up to me from San Francisco by the new Courts in that district. I have been ordered to secure the premises of Hampton's Emporium for the interests of two businessmen in the port. Seems Mister Charlie here gave a few Notes around, but this one is older than Missus Sunny's paper, which I do not disbelieve.'

'Like I said Sheriff. Case dismissed and issue decided.' Judge Perkins got to his feet, dusted off his lap, and clumped out of the store. And although the outcome seemed a happy one, all would agree, the Sheriff was not a satisfied man. He made a little whistling noise as he placed his hand upon his breast, just above his heart's place. Then, without a word spoken, he pressed through the crowd and went outside.

Then came the fateful day, Fourth of July, 1852. Charlie and Sunny had decided to sell all the goods to satisfy the men in San Francisco and to start anew, with Sunny, far the better merchant, as owner and Charlie B. as clerk. But Sheriff Lockhart had decided that the store was not to open as he had a valid lien on the goods which he was bound to execute.

In the days before the Fourth, activity in Hampton's store was brisk, although the doors were shuttered as the two merchants together worked to place the goods in a favorable and tidy light. Charlie let it be known that no man would stop his sale of goods. Sheriff Lockhart was himself all up and down the main track of Weaverville astride his big chestnut; his curiosity and wariness combined to ratchet up the tension in the town with each pass he made. By the Fourth, it was as if Sunny and Lockhart were on the whizzing path of planets about to fall into the sun.

At one o'clock in the afternoon, Charlie unshuttered his place and waited for the customers to assemble for the special sale, the morning celebrations having long concluded with a flapjack breakfast in the gambling tent and free coffee for all. Before the townsmen could come up to trade, Sheriff Lockhart and a posse of seven men from the camp over at the Hay Fork River approached the Emporium head on.

I watched from behind the dry store's barrels at the far side of the place as Charlie Hampton, drew out his Colt's firearm from under the wooden counter where the gun was hidden, next to the cash box. He held it in his right hand, the pistol barrel pointing to the dirt floor. His gaze was fixed on the opened doorway. Outside, the air was heavy with summer dust and the eight men standing in the road, the Trinity County Sheriff and his posse, remained poised in the hazy heat, resting on the heels of their boots. None of them, neither Sheriff Lockhart, nor any of his men, could make eye contact with Hampton, as each was wearing a repeat of a steep crowned, dark hat with a wide brim. In the savage light of the July noonday, their eyes were obscured. It was Justice blindfolded.

The man at the counter cocked the pistol, now, and aimed it toward the Sheriff, raised it in a graceful arc, as if he were gesturing on the stage. I do believe he only meant it as a warning.

Sunny stood a few feet away from Charlie; her own gun, a bone handled Derringer, was also cocked and ready in her hand, hidden in the folds of her best serge gown. She had been to the patriotic celebration winding up under the great white tent of the casino. Her bonnet, a black moire affair, was still on her head, the ribbons loose around her face, and in her ears, rubies set in gold glinted in the hard light. Behind the posse, an ominous shimmer lay on the dry hillside and heat-stunned insects swam through thick air.

After the deed was done, no one remembered who fired first. It may have been Sunny. She was known to pick her apples before they were

95

sweet. As the seconds ticked by, the suspense had become so fierce, the silence so insistent, that an indrawn breath, or even the rearrangement of a finger on a gun stock, could have precipitated the fusillade. Once the firing had begun, shots in quick succession riddled the stocky man behind the counter and his body deflated where he stood, falling over in a pool of gore and flesh and brains. Sunny's breast was torn apart where she took the loads of buckshot that sprayed from the posse's rifles. She fell, face down, her dark auburn hair soon soaked in the blood that ran freely from beneath her body. Her black bonnet rolled into the corner and stopped, covered with dust. Neither the Sheriff, nor any of his men, was hit.

All present later swore that the Sheriff never fired at the woman. It was the others, they said, the men in the posse, that killed her.

She had come into this world as Julia O'Hurley, from around Barleycove in the County Cork, and had acquired her pet name on the ship over from Queenstown. She had a smile that changed her face into a very sunrise, a smile that was hard to read because it always looked like genuine pleasure. I was to know her in her more private hours and I can tell you, she did not savor much happiness in her life. But because those she smiled on saw only pleasure in her eyes, they took to calling her Sunny. Proof, again, that fellow creatures only see what fancies dwell inside themselves.

The two, Hampton and Sunny, side by side, were laid to their heavenly rest in a piece of derelict earth just outside the town, no church or burial ground having yet been built. But when Father Wilhelm Florian came to town and blessed the new built Church of the Holy Trinity, Sunny, in her graveclothes, was moved to the sanctified soil of her childhood beliefs. A few years later, miners still around who remembered that sad and bloody day collected enough funds to place a sandstone marker on her grave. But it did not survive a year when some small minded women in the church had the marker taken down for want of decency. They did have the charity to leave Sunny to her rest.

The Sheriff kept at his post for half a year. People were polite, but their eyes could not hold his fierce and darkening gaze. He seemed a dangerous soul. Without warning, he quit his office and went off alone, deep into Humboldt County, up where the diggings were slim, but the big game was plentiful. Then, while hunting elk with a companion new to California, he placed his gun atop a fallen redwood. The companion, a trapper from the Upper Missouri, reported that Lockhart had stopped to examine the oyster mushrooms that grew along the seams of the fallen tree. When Lockhart went to regain his weapon, it was said the hammer tangled with a knot and the gun was discharged, dealing a fatal blow. It was a strange account and there were those who believed more lay behind this story, but no man made to enquire further. At the time of his death, Lockhart was thirty seven years old, six foot three inches tall and weighed about two hundred and twenty pounds, according to the record issued by the Coroner of Humboldt County. He had black eyes and whiskers the same.

For myself, I left the Valley of the Trinity and travelled to Eureka; the sporting houses in Weaverville had been forced more and more out of sight, to the less visible regions behind the hills. I preferred to be in the middle of things. In Eureka, I met a sailor man and voyaged with him up to Cape Flattery, the rocky sentinel that marks the great Straits that are named for Spanish adventurers of long ago. We find this pleasant shore is choked with trees two times as thick around as the trees in the Trinity Valley. There seems no limit to their number.

The Monkey

Imogen Robertson

From: Stephen Randle to Frederick Sheppard

'The Ship', Scarborough.

August 15, 1809.

Dear Frederick,

Well, my dear friend, as you see from the fine note paper borrowed from the establishment, I am now settled in 'The Ship', and shall kick my heels here till things quieten down a little in town. It is hard, Frederick, to be ever in want of the most basic necessities of life. The allowance my father makes me would not clothe an ostler, yet I must dress and go about me in the world, as you know. You have no idea how lucky you are to be your own master in matters of money.

Still, the old man, to do him justice, has dealt with the most persistent or well connected of my creditors, and here I am secluded from all the temptations of the town till he sees fit to forgive me, or at least allow me back into his august presence for another series of improving lectures. He has a nasty habit of pleading our poverty, and asks me if I would like to see my sister portionless and dependant on her friends! Though I was careful not to say so, I believe it would suit her temperament exactly. One as careful as she is, to be always so good, and obliging, and grateful, could not be but welcome in a dozen houses in Kent, and if they would only allow me half of what has been set aside for her marriage portion to dress and move about in the town, I could find me à pretty little wife with £30,000 to her name. I did consider putting this to him in the nature of an investment, but he was his most grave and awful, so I held my peace.

I would mind less being sent into obscurity at this time were it not for the fact I have been making great progress in the affections of Miss

Harding. She has no family of course, other than trade, but they are coming it rather high this season and I have every reason to believe her fortune would keep us all very happily for a good many years. I have spent the last three weeks sighing over her music, clutching my breast with emotion on seeing her rather inept watercolours of the Lake District, and reading a great deal of poetry to her in my most affecting tones. I think she is a fairly good way to being in love with me, and I am most fond of her father's money. I am convinced we should get along admirably.

Mr. Harding however does not like me, no matter how I try and seduce him by talking of the 'change and nodding wisely at everything he says. Perhaps he sees me too much with his daughter, where everything must be sentiment. Still, it is hard indeed to be pulled away from London at this delicate juncture. Who knows what fool will worm himself into my place while I am away. However, Papa was very strict and Mama cried, so I must play the penitent a little while and write them long letters about how quietly I am living, though in a slightly different tone from this to you.

I have given it out in town and here that I am touring the area for my health, and have let fall, most delicately, hints of my expertise in the world of art and design. If another such adventure as Plymouth were to occur I could be back in London within the week with pockets well lined. The ignorance of that young man made me £40 in the final reckoning. He will no doubt smart if he ever learns what a foolish bargain he made, but he is richer than I and a great deal more stupid, so I have no regrets. The likelihood of any gem appearing in the guise of an unloved conversation piece here is rather unlikely of course, but it does my heart good to dream of the possibility.

I hope your pursuit of Miss Alsop proceeds without any of the interruptions my campaign with Miss Harding has suffered. Really, Fred, in your last letter you sounded quite plausibly in love! Be careful you do not so far indulge in those tender emotions, that if you come to settlement and find her fortune dwindles to less than a sufficiency, you still insist on the lady and marry for affection. It would be a tragic thing to die in practice, scrounging to feed your children I think, rather than with your feet up by the fires of a nice little place in the country.

Send me whatever news you can, and anything to make me laugh. The latest fooleries of Tom Padgett over Ripley's old whore would suit very well. I think I shall die of boredom here, and my bones be picked over by seagulls before any of my friends think to enquire.

Your affectionate friend,
                              Stephen

                                        'The Ship', Scarborough.
                                        August 30, 1809.

Dear Frederick,

Pray, my good friend, do not be so quick to find offence. You are grown so upright under the charms of your lady, I hardly know you for the man who once shook Venice with such vigour I was sure the whole city would come loose and sink. I am sure, when paying attentions to Miss Alsop you think only of her many admirable qualities, yet I think she will make a more comfortable wife than a lady with the same qualities and a smaller fortune. Perhaps while your senses have been refined by the warm tones of your gentle companion, mine have been blunted by the evermore discordant cries of parents and creditors. Yes, of course the duty of an estate is noble work for an English gentleman, and I will gladly shoulder it when that time arrives. But why should I waste the best years of my life trying to free the land of debt by means of the law or any other profession you are so kind as to suggest, when I might gather the same capital in an instant by means of a wife?

However I must leave off apologising and debating with you here as I have a rather wonderful tale to tell, and can no longer bear with patience spending my paper in argument, when I should be sharing it.

I was, it seems, too quick to judge this little town as lacking anything worth looking at. My good hostess at 'The Ship' has seen fit to mention to her neighbours and other customers that there is a gentleman staying in the inn, by which she means myself of course, terribly wise about all sorts of art and always ready to see something interesting. Thus I caught a very pretty fish that may swim me back to town! After dinner yesterday as I read through your rather dull letter (not a word about Padgett, I think you quite cruel), a lady and her two girls were shown into my private parlour carrying an interesting package between them, wrapped in a rather tatty shawl. I say between them, but really it was the mother of the little tribe that was doing the carrying. The eldest girl, ten perhaps, kept grabbing at it, calling it hers and weeping for it, till the lady had to put her outside the door and into the care of Mrs. Peters, and I say 'Lady', my dear Fred, because I am more of a gentleman than you think. She was dressed very shabbily. Of the younger daughter I can say little, because she did nothing but slump in the far corner of the room for the duration of the visit, and cough.

Well, I had little notion of there being anything of great merit wrapped in the shawl, and still less when I heard the woman speak, torturing our English tongue with the local vowels. Her husband, dearly missed and departed for a better place, though whether that better place is in this world or another she did not say, was a sailor, and had apparently bought the contents of the shawl home from China, where the good local merchants at one point sent him. It was given, she admitted, as a special gift to the elder child, but without his support their need was such … (Did I mention she spent a lot of this speech coughing too? Do not worry on my account however, I had the windows open and the fires lit as soon as they were out of the place, and you know I am as healthy as a horse). Yes, such was their need they must to sell the toy of one to feed all three. The father always called the eldest his little monkey, and bought her this other to keep her company.

Well, I waited for the package to be opened, expecting a child's toy of some sort, but what joy! Under that rag of material lay one of the prettiest ivories it has ever been my pleasure to look upon. It is of a monkey, seated rather like a man, perhaps six inches tall, with its arms lightly folded on its lap and its lips parted showing a row of perfectly carved teeth in what seems to be a broad and well meaning laugh. I would judge it as coming from somewhere in the middle of the last century. Nothing so remarkable in the subject or date, you'll say, but the quality of the carving, Fred! It breathes! Its animal pelt, its sharp little eyes! I promise you my friend, you expect him to get up from his stool and start swinging around the room at any moment. I am surprised a thing of such delicacy survived the ownership of a child, but it is perfect! It was an honour and pleasure to hold the little creature. I am glad to say I kept all signs of surprise to myself however, merely lifted the little thing to my nose and peered at it with some humming and hawing till I was all but cross-eyed, and the woman standing in front of me all the while, atremble as to what the great man might say!

When I felt I had carried this on as long as necessary, I sat the thing down on the table in front of me as casually as I would my mother's second best tea things, and pronounced with a drawl:

'A pretty little thing, but I fear you have deceived yourself if you think it is of any great value. I could perhaps sell it for a pound in London if I were to find someone whose tastes tend that way, but that is all. You had much better give it back to your daughter.'

Dear Fred, the emotions that passed over the woman's face during my little speech were so transparent as to be almost comic! First despondency, then her eyes widening with hope as I mentioned the dizzying riches of a pound, then confusion and despair as I pushed it back towards her.

'Sir,' she says, trying hard to hold herself straight, 'you would be doing a great kindness if you were to buy it from me for one of your friends. I must feed the children until I am well enough to work again, and a pound would make all the difference to us.'

I made the face a man might make if he were tugged in one direction by his good heart, and in the other by his disinclination to make a bad deal. So she pipes up again.

'But, Sir, I am presuming. Perhaps if you were to give me fifteen shillings for it, the difference might make some recompense for your kindness and trouble.'

Well I could not resist that, a figure for which any dealer in London would give £600 and his right hand, for 15 shillings! So I smiled and agreed, and she was pathetically grateful.

Ahh, now you think me a wretch to take advantage in this way and will never deal with me again. Well do not be so hasty to judge, my friend. So pleased was I, with both the deal concluded and the new and interesting character of a gentleman philanthropist she had thrust up on me, I gave her the full 20 shillings! What do you say to that? I murmured something about 'feeling for her position', and possibly a word on 'our brave sailors'. I thought I might have gone too far, but not a touch! You would have thought I had miraculously healed the whole family by her reaction. You still feel badly for them? Well, I cannot allow you to do so. A pound, you know is just the amount of money that will change their lives materially for the better, and £600 is just the amount that will do the same for me, so you see we have both benefited from the exchange in equal measure. Have I not the right of it?

It is true the little owner of the statue was not so pleased as the rest of us. As the woman and her coughing child were taking their leave, quite obviously without the little parcel, the elder one lunged away from Mrs. Peters and shouted right in my face.

'You are a bad man! Very bad! The monkey does not like you! He does not like you at all!'

Quite the little devil, she was. Her mother hurried her away before she had the chance to do more than give me a comically angry look from under her fierce little brows. I think it rather unfair, as it was her mother that did the selling after all, but to her she made no reproach. I almost regretted those five extra shillings, for, apart from her very red eyes, that child at least looked to be in rude health.

So off they go into the warren of streets from which they came, to sink or swim as the Almighty sees fit, and I while away the time till the next London stage departs writing to you with the little monkey looking over my work. I could grow quite fond of him. Be certain of it, in a month from now you will be wishing me and Miss Harding joy, and this little fellow will have pride of place in one of the better collections of London. How neatly things can come round!

Your affectionate friend,

Stephen

Seven Dials, London
September 5, 1809

Dear Frederick,

How sorry I am you are not currently in town, but if you must race off all over the country in pursuit of a certain lady's glances, I know better than to try and prevent you for the sake of mere friendship. I hope Bath agrees with you. I thank you for your good wishes and indeed I am a lucky man, but I find my return to London has not been the triumphal entry I had hoped for.

It began well enough. I was only an hour off the stage when I succeeded in meeting with Sir Thomas Betteridge just outside my father's club. Indeed, I had gone there in search of Sir Thomas as the most likely man to truly appreciate my monkey friend, but was nervous of entering and so allowing reports of my return from exile to reach my father's ears. It was lucky indeed then, that he emerged just as I was hesitating on the doorstep. I let him have a swift look at my little friend even there on the street, and such was his excitement we hurried to his home in Hanover Square in half the usual time. I knew he was mine before the carving was fully unwrapped (you'll be glad to know the shawl was abandoned in Scarborough and the monkey is now wrapped in good felt). He had that look of hunger on his face that denotes a truly greedy connoisseur. I mean the remark as a compliment of course.

He said everything that was proper and agreed that my price was reasonable without demure (on consideration I thought £700 a proper figure), yet just when we were comfortably set, and even as our hands were clasped he confessed he did not have anything like the sum available in ready money and begged me to wait ten days for him to gather the necessary. Sir Thomas in want of ready money! The man who makes Croesus look a pauper! I could not have been more surprised if the King himself had walked into the room and asked to borrow my handkerchief. Yet his manner was sincere, and he was most urgent in his wish that I offer the carving nowhere else. A most unlucky combination of circumstances it appears, some investments recently made, other opportunities arising and his eldest daughter's late marriage. However he was intent on giving me some ten pounds to secure my promise I would not sell the creature before the date stated. Very well, I am resolved to wait till then, eight days from now, and in the meantime I have taken two little rooms in a rather dank corner, as you may see from my address, am avoiding any places where Papa or his associates might to be found, and am relying on the next door chop house for my sustenance.

I could not resist though going to pay a call on Miss Harding, in a very quiet way, the following morning, and there, dear Fred, I have found still more to vex me. Rather than the comfort of a joyful welcome and a series of meaningful looks sought and exchanged, she was oddly cold and nervous with me. It seems I am out of favour, yet how I cannot tell. When I endeavoured to give her a look, a word of more significance, she looked at me with something like horror. Of course I am not in love with the lady, so my heart is in no danger from this strange behaviour, but I have been something like in love with the visions of a future made comfortable and secure by our alliance. I was really quite distressed.

The walk back to my rooms was most unpleasant, the weather warm, the air stinking and every man, woman and child on the road taking turns to buffet me from one side of the pavement to the other. When I got the door safely closed behind me, I realised some of the pushes had had more mischief in them than others. My father's watch was taken, which feels like a sad blow. How our spirits effect what our eyes see in the world. When I looked at the carving set up on table in front of me as I patted my coats with increasing dismay, instead of the bright laugh I had seen at first on its face, I saw rather a sneer. It looked to me as if I had been judged by the beast and found wanting. The heat of the day, conspiring with the warmth of my feelings, and the fierce exercise of a considerable walk undertaken rather quicker than was necessary, had given me a headache that now thundered in my skull. The little beast and I looked one another in the eye and all I could hear was the chant of that wretched sailor's daughter 'The monkey does not like you! The monkey does not like you!'

I fell into my bed at last and awoke in the evening feeling quite calm again. The lady is testing me perhaps, and though it is a great shame that I can not take Sir Thomas's money at once, I have the promise of it in eight days.

I was comforted, yet these reverses seem to have had some effect on my nerves. I have been sleeping ill, starting at every sound, of which of course there are many in an establishment such as this, and at times I awake with the conviction that there is a stuttering, a pattering coming from within the room itself.

I reassure myself that this nervousness will pass the moment that Sir Thomas's bills are in my hand. It can not come a moment too soon. I am too much in this room, and too much under the eyes of this malevolent little beast.

Your friend,
Stephen

Seven Dials.
September 11, 1809.

Dear Frederick,

Thank you for your concern, my dear friend. I wish I could give you a better account of myself.

The night of my last letter to you I ordered supper in my rooms and drowned my disappointments in the landlady's worst burgundy. I thought by drinking myself insensible I might free myself of the little noises in the room that had made my previous night's rest so uncomfortable. It was a bad miscalculation on my part. I dreamt. So much I might share with any man, but what a dream! I can hardly bear to tell it. I seemed to be in my bed, and seemed to be woken by the chant of the sailor's daughter inside my mind, and a chattering animal laugh. I seemed to stand, I say seemed, but it felt as real, more real than the world that surrounds me now. I lit my candle and made my way into the parlour. I was looking for the monkey in its usual place on the table. I cannot convey the horror, Fred, the lurch in my soul, when I saw that the monkey was gone. Never for a moment did I think, as I would in my rational, waking self, that the figure had been stolen or removed. As I stood there I knew the monkey was free and in the room, and stepping forward I caught sight of the little ivory stump on which the figure usually sits.

The scuttering sound began, and I knew, absolutely knew, whatever I had told myself on previous nights, it was the monkey and it meant me harm. I saw a movement to my right in the shadows and turned with a cry to face it, then a moment later I heard the noise again on my left. Again I turned my candle towards it, again I saw nothing but the usual furniture of the room and the shadows from my feeble light.

Breathing deeply, I began to make a slow arc with my candle across the room. Oh, Fred! It sounds a nonsense of wine and over-stretched nerves, yet I am weak with fear even as I narrate! The light reached slowly the centre area of the parlour floor. There he was. Animate. Conscious. Staring at me with such concentration of purpose. My heart, I am sure, stopped for a moment as I looked into his little white eyes. Then I felt my anger rise from my belly. I hated the tiny white monster at that moment more than I have ever hated anything in my life. I blamed it for all my misfortunes and, with deliberate loathing, I drew back my foot to kick the horrible beast back into hell. It raised itself off its haunches and hissed at me through its tiny ivory teeth. My candle fluttered and went out.

For a moment everything was dark, the silence complete, then I heard the roar of an angry beast at my back and closer to me than this paper is to the pen. I felt the cool animal air of it, but almost before the sensation was recognised a huge, strong and violent hand seized me by the shoulder and threw me to the floor.

Oh God! The horror of that moment. My terror was absolute. In the moonlight I saw the ivory head of the monkey, now grown to be somewhat larger than that of a man, its teeth bared, its jaws wide open in rage, its white body rippling with muscle. It crouched above my body, holding me powerless to the floorboards then screamed at me, and lifted its head I believe to bite through my unhappy neck! And in my brain always the same chant, 'The monkey does not like you! The monkey does not like you!' in the hurt and angry voice of the cheated child. I lost consciousness, and awoke in the full light of day and in my own bed.

Oh Frederick, every night since, as soon as I close my eyes some variation on that terrible theme is played! I have become an old man in a few days. I grow thin and cannot conceal a tremble in my hand. The madness of the night begins to infect my waking hours, and every face I see seems to reflect something of the monkey or the little girl. I am caught by my accusers everywhere!

It was madness to visit Miss Harding in this state, but I wished for some comfort, and hoped she might take pity upon me. It was a most uncomfortable morning, beginning badly and ending far more bitterly. She greeted me as coldly as before and in all her looks and replies were readable the unmistakeable signs of a person trying to overcome a visceral aversion in the name of good manners. This, from the lady of whom I had such hopes! My smile once brought the roses to her cheek in an instant, so many moments I could recall in that very room of such delightful consciousness!

I am ashamed to say I grew warm, found myself demanding an explanation from her; Oh the chill in her voice as she said:

'I cannot say, Sir. But I no longer feel the pleasure in your company I once did. I ask you to forgive me.'

She turned away and I took hold of her arm. She gave a little cry. I thrust my face into hers, insisted again that she had loved me, called her … Oh Frederick, I shall never repeat what I said, but it was unjust and very, very wrong of me. Her cry brought her father into the room, and so he found me bruising his daughter's arm and her in a fit of frightened tears.

I was abruptly thrown from the house. The footman who shoved me from the door did so with enough indignant force to tumble me down the steps and into the gutter, much to the amusement of the common people passing. I cannot blame him.

So I returned to the malicious glee of the monkey. I hear him almost continually now, that evil chattering laugh with which the nightmare begins. My one comfort, the one notion that prevents me sinking entirely, is that in two days time the thing will be gone, and I can begin to repair the damage he has caused.

Your unfortunate friend,
Stephen

Seven Dials.
September 13, 1809.

Frederick,

I am cursed! Sir Thomas still has not the money!

I set out from this place with such feverish joy this morning, the world seemed unnaturally bright, my manner, I know, was over-engaged. But the knowledge that I was about to be free was intoxicating. I was outside his house while the maids were still asleep and must have turned a thousand times around the square before the first possible moment for a visit had arrived. I was shown straight into his room of business and I cannot tell you the panic that gripped my heart as I heard him speak.

'I am most ashamed, Sir, to have promised and not be able to fulfil that promise. This has been the most extraordinary chain of circumstance, and while I seem to have suffered no great loss of fortune, it means I can not lay my hands on so much as fifty pounds today, let alone seven hundred.'

I staggered as I stood before him. He leapt up to take my arm.

'You are not well, Sir!' he says, and tries to lead me to a chair, but such was the panic in my soul I would not be forced down, my only thought was that I must be rid of the thing at once, I could wait for his money no longer. I rushed headlong from his house and dashed blindly down Bond Street to the showroom of Abel Crane. I knew his terms would be less generous than those of Sir Thomas, but I could not endure the thought of another night with the creature in my possession.

My appearance must have been ghastly, but he welcomed me in with the courtesy of an old acquaintance. I scarcely stuttered through the civilities necessary and put the figurine on the table in front of me. He took it up with a cry of pleasure that gave me hope, and examined it happily for a minute, then a change began to steal over his face. He frowned.

'I do not like it, Mr. Randle. The carving is exquisite, and the subject charming. I cannot explain my dislike, and I do not understand it. But I have learnt, by living so long, that sometimes our hearts and souls understand deeper truths that our minds do not. Therefore I can only tell you I do not like it, and ask you to remove it from my establishment.'

'For one hundred pounds, Mr. Crane! You know it is worth ten times as much,' I cried, lurching forward in my chair. He shook his great round head gravely at me.

'I know it to be worth at least a seven or eight hundred, but I would not buy it for a shilling. I ask you again, Sir. Please remove it from my house.'

I could not speak, but staggered from the door.

On Bond Street I put my hand in my pocket and squeezed the figurine, scarcely caring if I snapped it, and I felt a sharp sting. When I withdrew my hand I saw that the forefinger was marked by a neat semicircle of teeth marks. I pulled the monkey from my pocket, determined in that moment to throw it into the sewer, but caught site of myself in the plate windows of the building opposite and was horrified. Mad, quite mad.

I have come home. The monkey is swaddled and I must wait for Sir Thomas to gather his money. I know I can survive a few more days. Dear Frederick, I wish you were here to advise me.

Stephen

Seven Dials.
September 17, 1809

My dear, dear Frederick,

I shall never be able to thank you enough for your care, your generosity and your advice so freely given over the last few days. I owe you my life. I still have no memory of your arrival I fear, and I shudder to think what I must have seemed to you then. My first memory is of waking in the night, and seeing your dear face watching over me. Your wife will be blessed in you indeed, but if a very little of what you say is her is true, she deserves you. I have done exactly as you directed. The figurine has been carefully packed up and entrusted to the driver of the Scarborough stage to be deliver to Mrs. Peters at 'The Ship', and a civil note with it requesting she see it to its former owners.

The air in the room here seems lighter and cleaner already, and I have slept peacefully. I thank you my friend, and I shall show my thanks by my actions as well as my words. Your goodness has humbled me, and my sins weigh heavily on my conscience. I will make peace with my father and learn to be a better man than I have been.

My compliments and respects to Miss Alsop, I look forward to the acquaintance with great pleasure.

Your grateful friend, and humble servant,

Stephen Randle

From: Mrs. Sophia Peters to Mr. Stephen Randle

'The Ship', Scarborough

September 20, 1809

Dear Sir,

I indeed remember you very well, and I thank you for your kind wishes and compliments, but I am sorry to say it is out of my power to assist you.

The day before your package arrived, I had the sad duty of attending the funeral of the lady in question. She followed her youngest to the grave in quick order and I believe, Sir, when you met them they were already past help. The eldest girl you mention, is called Harriet, but at the last sight I had of her, she was being taken away by her mother's sister. Their home is in Weybridge I believe, and I understand the aunt to be a respectable woman of the name of Miller, though she already has six little ones of her own, so I doubt she was mighty pleased to take on another. I do not have any further direction for them or the resources to discover it. I thought it best then to return the little monkey to you, the same way it came.

I regret I cannot be of more help in this matter and remain, Sir,

Your humble servant,

Sophia Peters (Mrs.)

Seven Dials

Frederick,

It is returned. I cannot any longer ... It seeks its revenge, Frederick, all my resolves are come to nothing. May God have mercy on me!

unsigned

From The London Times, September 28, 1809
'Strange and Tragic Death in Seven Dials'

On the morning of the 26th September the household of Mrs. Clorinda Masterson was awoken very early by a gentleman who demanded entrance to the rooms there rented by a Mr. Stephen Randle, saying he believed his friend to be in some distress. Thus roused, Mrs. Masterson tried to call her tenant. On receiving no answer, and yielding to the impassioned requests of the gentleman's friend, they forced the door, and opened it on a tragic and horrific scene. The furniture and linen of the place had been cast about as if in a mighty struggle, and the unfortunate resident was found dead on the floor. He had suffered a mortal wound to the throat, but as the door to the chamber was locked from within and the windows closed, how he came by it remains a mystery. Any persons with knowledge of this strange and unpleasant crime should report with all due haste to the house in Bow Street any morning between ten and midday.

From: Mrs. Elizabeth Miller to Mr. Frederick Sheppard

Weybridge, December 14, 1809

Dear Sir,

I am glad you continue to be pleased with little Harriet, and I am very happy to agree to your taking full charge of her, knowing all the advantages that a genteel education can offer. I hope she realises what a lucky girl she is. It was a wonderful thing to see how she took to yourself and your dear lady, even before you handed her back her little toy. She slept with it in her hand all that night and I am sure she does so still.

Did I tell you of her first response when I told her of your kind offer? She was quiet for a little while, then said.

'Yes, Aunt. I shall go and stay with the gentleman and lady. We are too many for you here, and the monkey likes him.'

Such a way she has, Sir. I'm sure you must be overjoyed to hear her toy approves of you!

My thanks also and those of my husband for the mention you made of our youngest boy Samuel to Captain Travers-Brown. Sam sails in a month from now, and we could not be more happy or proud.

You, your wife and Harriet will remain forever in the prayers of your obedient servant,

Elizabeth Miller.

Refugees

Janette Walkinshaw

The men came in the early morning, while we were at Terce.

They came from Dumfries, riding up the side of the River Nith to where it joined with our own Cluden Water.

Sister Catherine heard them first. I felt her stiffen beside me and lift her head, and pause in her singing. Then I heard them too, a click of metal hoof on the cobblestones of the courtyard, and the murmur of men's voices, and then silence. They were waiting.

I felt maggots crawling in my belly.

Mother Prioress hadn't heard. Neither had Sister Theresa, who was watching the way her breath fluttered the candle in front of her, a vacant expression on her face. I could tell by the movement of her lips that she was singing the wrong words, or no words at all.

Gloria in excelsis deo et in terra pax hominus bonae.

Our singing was thin, lost in the dark cold of the chapel. Mother sang the Amen slowly. There was silence save for the guttering noise of the tallow candles. The whole Priory stank of this tallow. It was all we had, after Sister Judith died of the black death, and the bees swarmed and were taken by others.

Mother rose from her knees. Sister Catherine's hand under her elbow was gentle, for touching Mother caused her pain.

Outside, the sun was barely above the horizon. The men had turned their horses onto the stubble of the barley field, and were lounging in the courtyard. They straightened up as we approached. One man turned and spat into the well.

"Lady Blanche," the Steward greeted Mother.

"You have a message for us."

"I have to do it," he said.

She nodded to him and we waited.

He took the parchment from his pouch and read it aloud.

To his Holiness Pope Clement. From his Grace the Earl Archibald Douglas, Lord of Galloway. This the twenty third day of September in the year of our Lord One thousand three hundred and eighty nine. Concerning the nuns of Lincluden Priory.

A petition that the said Priory be closed and the nuns moved elsewhere. These women have now taken to leading dissolute and scandalous lives, allowing the beautiful monastic buildings to fall into disrepair and ruin through neglect, while they dress their daughters, born in incest, in silk with gold ornaments and pearls.

"That's not true," I cried.

He paused and caught my eye. I should have lowered my head, as all my life I had done in the presence of strangers, but I did not. I stared back at him.

"Go on," said Mother.

"You could take the rest as read."

"No," said Mother. "Go on."

He went on with his reading.

The number of nuns including the prioress is reduced to four and they neglect the observances of the day and night offices, devoting their time to the spinning of wool. The local neighbours, who are very evil men, repair to the monastery in order to defend themselves from the enemies of Scotland, being situated on the borders, or to a house about a mile distant from It, where they hold a market and even commit incest.

I saw Mother close her eyes for a moment. I saw Catherine looking bewildered. Theresa, as usual, had disappeared.

"It is God's will," said Mother.

I was speechless with anger.

The steward rolled up his script. "The consent has come from the Holy Father. Your priory is to be closed."

The men left. "One week," said the Steward.

Later that day, I walked into Dumfries.

I found Baillie McBraer in conversation with the mason.

The new castle they were building to defend the town against the

English already rose four storeys high, the thick walls nearly complete. As I approached, another block of red sandstone was being raised, pulled up by a windlass on top of the wooden scaffolding.

Baillie McBraer saw me, and with a word dismissed the mason.

"Sister."

"Baillie. I've come about the payment for the barley. We are in need of it now."

"Oh, aye. A moment, lady." He turned to give a signal to some men manoeuvring a cart with more stones in it. "Further over," he called out. "Give me two minutes, I'll be with you."

He turned back to me. "Do you like our new castle, Sister. A fine building."

"The English will find it hard to burn," I said.

Baillie McBraer made a derisory noise in his throat.

"English. They'll not come over the border again. Not now Lord Archibald has shown them they can't do it. A brave soldier, Sister, just like his father before him. But if they do come back," he waved his hand in the direction of the building work. "We'll be ready for them."

It was not many years since I stood with my sisters at the gate of Lincluden Priory and watched Dumfries burning. The people came upriver to us for refuge. We took the women and girls and the babies inside. The men, such few old men and boys as were left from the wars, camped outside in the shelter of our walls.

For several days we waited, quietly, with the townspeople, watching the clouds glowing red while their timber and thatched houses burned.

Easy burnt, easy built, I remember one woman saying. Happened before, it'll happen again.

Our priory was stone, and we thought it would stand forever.

The Baillie turned back to look at the men working on the castle, signalling to them with snapping fingers.

I persisted. "Baillie, may I have the payment for our grain?"

"Oh that. Might be a bit of a problem paying you."

"There must be something due to us. There were twenty bushels."

"But, but, it's like this. I'm told you'll all be leaving the priory, sister. The Earl's intending to enlarge it, turn it into an abbey, I hear, for monks.

They're to say prayers in perpetuity for his ancestors. Yes. Well by rights the money belongs to them. I mean, it's not your money personally, is it? You've taken vows of poverty. You'll be going to a new convent, and they'll have received the money for their grain. I couldn't pay it to you, that would be like you getting the money twice. D'you see that?"

I thought of the hours spent turning over the soil, and sowing the barley, and the back-breaking labour we'd had of bringing it in.

Perhaps I should have pleaded. Perhaps he wanted me to plead. But I was too proud.

"I'll let Earl Archibald know I'm holding the money. It's here for his new abbot."

He signalled to the men who were waiting.

"Good day to you, Sister."

"God with you," I replied, automatically.

As I walked back through the town, I heard people laughing. Men shouted lewd words at me. Once they would not have dared. I walked out of the town, my cheeks burning, trembling with anger.

I knew that when the priest came I should confess this, for anger is a sin, but the priest never came. He used to come once a week to the Priory to say Mass and hear our confession, but after this we never saw him again.

During the week that was left to us Sister Catherine, Sister Theresa and I sorted through the few clothes we had, and chose the warmest, and heavy woollen cloaks, and the best and soundest of our boots. We packed some food for the journey ahead of us.

Mother knelt at her stall in the chapel, praying, as long as she was able.

Catherine followed me around all the time. Every time I lifted my head from my task, there she would be, whitefaced and frightened.

"I have never lived anywhere but here."

She had come to the monastery as a baby. Her mother had been one of the many, oh so many women who had died of the plague. Catherine had survived and had been brought here, for there was no one to care for her.

I took her hand and held it.

"There will be somewhere for us. There will be another monastery, with Sisters of your own age, and we will be made welcome."

We were ready when the soldiers came a week later. They dragged our bedstraw out and the straw from the refectory, and burned it, laughing as they crushed the cockroaches underfoot. They took our cow and our handful of hens, and the pewter vessels from the chapel and the kitchen. Such silver as we had once had was long gone. They loaded everything that was in the priory onto bullock carts, and sent them away.

The four of us stood outside the walls and watched as they destroyed our home.

"What arrangements have been made for us," I asked the captain of the soldiers.

He did not know of any arrangements.

"But where are we to go?"

"I was told you had friends who would take you in."

"We have no friends. Not with the lies the Earl has been telling about us."

He shrugged. It was none of his business.

I was in despair.

Winter was nearly upon us. What were we to do?

It was no use going to Dumfries for help. Whether the people believed the Earl or not didn't matter. They would not take us in, for fear of his anger.

Mother was standing in the roadway, her eyes closed, praying. The two young girls waited by her side.

Mother opened her eyes. "We will go to Whithorn" she said. "To where the bones of the blessed St. Ninian lie in the cathedral. That will be our new home."

I argued. Whithorn was too far. It was a long way away, and winter was nearly on us. But Mother had faith. She had faith enough for all of us. When she was only a girl, she had left her family in the north to devote her life to the worship of God, and she knew He would not desert her now. How could I tell her that, God's help or not, she did not have the strength to walk anywhere? She did not see herself as stooped with age and crippled with rheumatism.

Besides, I had been taught to obey Mother Prioress in all things.

I wrapped her cloak more tightly round her.

Then Mother, who had not left the priory for over forty years, turned her face to the west, and picked her way carefully over the rutted track, without once looking back.

Catherine was crying, quietly, the tears pouring down her face.

Theresa said. "I'm not going."

"You must," I said. "There is nowhere else."

"There is," she said.

A lad was waiting in the road, dressed in poor rags, carrying a shepherd's crook. Theresa slung her pack from her back, and pulled out Mother's clothes, which I had given her to carry.

"Theresa, you don't know what you're doing."

She smirked at me. She patted her belly.

"Oh yes I do," she said. "Better than you."

I looked after the two of them, the boy and Sister Theresa, walk down the track together towards Dumfries, and realised how blind I had been.

Catherine was packing Mother's clothes into her own pack. She slung it on her back and followed after Mother.

"Where is Theresa going?" Mother asked.

Catherine answered before I could. "She has friends in the town. They will look after her."

"People are good," said Mother. "May the saints bless them."

I cut staffs for Mother and with one in each hand she was able to walk, but it was her needs which determined our pace.

At first our travel was not too difficult, for people still took their carts and beasts into Dumfries for the market there, and this had kept a road open, rutted and uneven though it was. But as we travelled away from Dumfries, into rougher country and towards the mountains, it became more difficult.

In places there were tracks, remnants of the old pilgrim road, but this was long disused, for there had been too many years of war. No one travelled now.

In the forests we were sheltered from the worst of the wind and rain, but the way was difficult and the going slow as we followed paths made by deer and rabbits to avoid undergrowth and bramble.

On the open moorland we stumbled our way through heather and bracken and learned that smooth ground was often treacherous, with unexpected black bogs into which we were sucked up to our knees.

We often had to climb higher to find a place where we could ford a fast flowing burn, and then slowly make our way again down the hillside, legs and shoulders aching.

We saw few people. Their houses were hidden in folds in the hills, and with winter coming they had taken their animals inside. Sometimes we saw wild goats, and deer, and heard the scream of a pheasant, but the land was almost deserted.

Sometimes we came across an empty ruinous house and we had shelter for the night and remnants of timber to build a fire. But often we had to sleep in the open, in the protection of trees, or under overhangs of rock.

Catherine fared best, being young and strong, and for many miles she would carry all the packs, while I supported Mother.

She and Mother never wavered in their confidence that we would reach Whithorn.

"Once," Mother told Catherine, "all the roads round about were black with pilgrims going to the shrine of St. Ninian. Thousands of pilgrims. They came by sea from Ireland and France and Spain. Some came from Flanders through England and walked this way, singing praises as they travelled."

"What's Whithorn like?" asked Catherine

"A great city. A great cathedral."

"And food?"

"A lot of food."

Catherine was always hungry. She would run ahead and dive into the woods through which we passed, searching for berries. She found brambles and blaeberries and gathered them in her kerchief, to share with us. She found mushrooms, which I added to the mess I cooked every night.

I kept us moving for already the air was cold, and the burns we had to cross sometimes had thin sheets of ice at the edges. I bullied and cajoled, and almost wept when Mother insisted we sing the Divine Office whenever she judged the hour was right. Inside I fumed at the waste of energy and the delays when we stopped, but what could I do?

At the end of each day every muscle and bone ached, till we could barely stand.

But as the days passed in a blur of exhaustion for us, and pain for her, soon our praise was only a prayer when we woke in the morning, and vespers before we settled to try and sleep. We did not sleep well. The ground was hard and when the fire died down it was cold. Sometimes in the night we heard wolves howling.

Our food was finished on the ninth day.

There came days when we walked with no food in our bellies. Sometimes Catherine found berries, but they were blackening with the cold, and scarce. Once a buzzard drop from the sky in front of us and we saw its talons close over a rabbit. We shouted and it dropped the rabbit and flew away, and the poor animal, injured and easily killed, gave us a good meal that night.

We had to keep walking, walking.

Each day we covered less and less ground. Mother's joints became swollen and hot to the touch. Each night I carefully took off her boots and massaged her feet.

Our boots, which had been made from the skin of our pig the year before and had seemed so strong at the priory, cracked and tore with the rain and the rough stones. Early on, I ripped up our wimples, and Mother's beautiful white cap, the badge of her office, to make rags to bind round our feet.

After that we wore our shawls over our shaven heads. Catherine's hair grew, and mine, but Mother's did not.

Mother and Catherine talked, while I lay silent and anxious.

"The good Lord and his mother will take care of us," I could hear Mother whispering. "And the good St. Ninian, he wants us there, where his bones are."

"Are we on the right road, Mother?" asked Catherine.

Mother had no doubts. We were to keep travelling west and we would arrive at the sanctuary of Whithorn.

We had been avoiding people, for shame that they knew our story, and fear that they would harm us. We had been told stories of outlaws in the hills, men who had deserted the fighting, and who would kill any travellers.

But we needed food, so we sought out people and we became beggars.

We came to a hamlet, no more than three or four houses beside a lochan, and I made the others wait in the shelter of some beech trees, out of sight.

I knocked at the first door and when it was opened a crack I asked for food.

"Be gone with you," the man shouted and banged the door closed.

I waited till I stopped shaking and approached another door. Two dogs ran out and one sank his teeth into my thigh. I screamed.

There was shouting from inside the house and a woman appeared. She called the dogs off.

"Goodwife, we are three women travelling the road to Whithorn. We have no food. Can we beg a crust?"

She shouted something incomprehensible at me, but it was not friendly.

I stood my ground and she shouted again, this time in a language I could understand.

"We have no food ourselves."

That night when Mother and Catherine were asleep I was able to rub salve into my leg. My clothes were thick, for we wove strong cloth in the priory, but my leg was badly bruised. And then I could allow myself some tears. The leg pained me for many days afterwards.

But many times people were kind, and gave us bread, and once some oatmeal, and the porridge I made that night filled our bellies and helped us to sleep.

The weather grew colder and the rain driving in from the north made everything wet and chill. There was nothing dry that would take a spark from my tinder, and often we did not have a fire. Mother suffered grievously.

At night I lay with her in my arms to keep her warm, and to cushion her old fleshless bones. I could hear the wheezing in her chest. It had been there for some days. The medicines I had carried for her were done, and there were no herbs to make up fresh.

My heart was full for I loved her as if she had been my real mother. She was my Mother in Christ, and I knew she was going to die.

Catherine and I made a sling with our joined hands. Mother sat in it with her arms round our necks, and we lifted her up and slowly, slowly, we felt our way, with shoulders and back and hips aching from the strain.

One day when I smelt peat burning I left the others and followed the smell till I came to a house of mud and stones and turves for a roof. There was no sign of anyone. From the byre there was a clatter and the constant bleat of a goat in heat.

Poor as they were, they had warmth and shelter and we had none.

I lifted the latch and opened the door cautiously. When there was no sound, no shout of protest, I entered. There was no one there. In one corner the peat fire smouldered, and my eyes smarted with the smoke which drifted across the room in the draught from the open door. When my eyes grew accustomed to the dimness I could make out the pallet bed in one corner, and the chair near the fire, and the spinning wheel and a fleece with the carder lying on top of it.

On a bench near the fire also there was some food. I stepped nearer. There was a piece of cheese wrapped in a cloth. Nearby was a tub and when I moved the straw which lay on the top I found that it contained apples.

The smell of the apples brought back the scent of the orchard at Lincluden and I lifted one and bit down hard on it, the juice running down my chin, and the pieces nearly choking me.

I grabbed the cheese, and filled my pockets with apples. There was also a bowl full of oatmeal, and I emptied this into my kerchief and knotted it. I ran out to where Mother and Catherine waited and hurried them away.

We had walked a short distance when we met a woman coming in the opposite direction. She was old and stooped and walked slowly, with a stick, and she was leading a stinking billy goat. She paused and would have spoken, I think, but I hurried the others on, save for a brief greeting.

I felt my sin grievously then, for she had the look of a woman who would have given us the food, and I prayed that when she found her house violated she would forgive these starving strangers.

Afterwards we all had stomach pains from the apples, but Catherine said it was better than the stomach pains from hunger.

The next morning Catherine woke soon after me. Mother was still asleep.

"The people there were kind," said Catherine.

"Where?"

"Back there. To give you so much food. Couldn't we go back and see if we can stay there for a while. We could work to earn our keep."

"No."

"Why not?"

"I stole the food."

There was silence, save for Mother's snoring.

"You stole it?"

"Yes, I stole it."

I caught the expression of disgust on her face.

"D'you think I'm proud of it? God knows, the woman had little enough."

"That was terrible."

"Would you rather starve to death?"

"What will Mother say when she finds out."

"She won't find out. You won't tell her."

"She'll say it's a sin."

"You will not tell her." I spoke the words slowly and gripped Catherine's arm as I spoke. She shook me off.

"Deo gratias, my daughters," Mother greeted us as usual when she woke.

"Deo gratias, Mother."

All that day I did not leave the two of them alone together.

The next morning, when I awoke, Catherine had gone.

I told Mother that she hoped to find a better road to Whithorn, and would come back to us if it was easier.

It was hard without Catherine.

The days had grown very short, for we were now nearly at the winter solstice, and the long, long nights were dark and cold. Sometimes, when Mother was asleep in my arms and I could not move for fear of disturbing her, I lay with my limbs numb and looked up at the stars, and thought

125

about Mother's enduring faith. She had no doubt that God and his son and St. Ninian were guiding us and protecting us on our journey, and with all of them to care for us, how could we come to harm?

Sometimes in the cold light of the moon, I saw shadows move, and heard sounds, and told myself they were only the night-time animals, but sometimes in my half-dozing state I could imagine them to be the goblins of legend come to get me. I remembered the stories of ghosts we used to tell in the priory when I was a girl. This annoyed the older nuns, who called us silly and superstitious. But I think they did it too when they were young. And surrounded by the safe stone walls of our priory, we could find the stories thrilling but meaningless. Now, they came back to me in all their horror.

I was always thankful when the first streaks of red began to lighten the sky in the east.

Then suddenly Catherine was there again.

I put my arms round her and she rested her head on my shoulder and we did not say anything for many minutes.

"Here," she said, unwrapping her pack. She handed me some bread, and some dried fish.

"And here," she said, and pulled out a phial. I opened it. Wintergreen. Other things. "Will this help Mother? Is it the right stuff?"

"It will ease her breathing."

Mother was still asleep. I held the phial under her nose and I rubbed some of it on her breast.

When she woke her breathing became easier and her eyes were brighter.

She cried to see Catherine back and clung to her,

We went on. Later, as we rested and ate and Mother dozed again, I asked Catherine, "Where did you get the food and the medicine?"

"Does it matter?"

I was instantly alert.

"Don't tell me you stole them."

"No, I paid for them."

"What with. You don't have anything."

She was silent. I reached out and twisted her arm. "What did you pay with."

She shook me off. "It was the only thing I had.

"I walked south for a long time after I left you. I was angry. What you did was a sin, and I thought I would rather die than commit such a sin. But I did not know that begging was so difficult. I tried it, but I was too frightened, and people looked too rough.

"I came to a house that stood by itself. There was a man milking a cow. He gave me a bowl of milk. Oh, Marjorie, do you remember the taste of warm milk, fresh from the cow? I thought I had never tasted anything so good and never would again.

"I could have gone on then, but I didn't. I could smell meat cooking inside the house, and it smelled so good, and I had been hungry for so long. He took me inside and gave me some of the meat. He had medicines too. Marjorie, I saw these things and knew they would help Mother.

"And I thought, I can no longer bear being hungry and cold, and I do not want to beg and I cannot steal, so I will have to pay for them.

"I put my arms round him. And he kissed me on the lips and I didn't know what to do after that, but he made me lie down on the bed and he did things to me, like an animal.

"He said afterwards he was sorry for I couldn't stop crying, and he helped me to clean myself up. But it wasn't his fault. I offered myself."

Her mouth twisted with the pain of telling it.

"His wife had died. His two sons had been taken for soldiers to fight the English and they never came back. He had fought too, in the service of Lord Archibald, and had been injured. He wanted me to stay.

"But then I ran away and found you again."

From time to time that night I heard her give a gulping sob, but she slept.

The next day Mother's breathing was easier. I carried her now. She was so light that I could lift her in my arms, and with Catherine leading the way to choose the easiest paths we made progress.

We no longer sang the praises of God.

And then we came to a glen, sheltered from the north wind.

In front of us in the gloaming we could see the bulk of a large building, with surrounding walls, and here and there the flicker of torches.

"Is this Whithorn?" asked Catherine.

We made our way to a torch burning in a sconce in the wall. This marked the location of the door, and beside it a bell gleamed in the light of the flame. I seized the clapper and rang the bell, and we waited.

The door opened and a man in the dress of a lay monk stood there.

"Where is this place?" I asked.

"Dundrennan Abbey."

Dundrennan, where the White Monks lived. We were a long way off our road. We must have come too far south, but I did not care.

I told him who we were.

"Wait," he said.

I had heard of this Abbey, spoken of with awe for the strictness of the Order. Their founder observed the most severe austerity, forgetting perhaps that our Lord Jesus had not lived in poverty, only in simplicity, and that what is right for the warm south is not necessarily suitable for a cold northern country.

We waited, shivering. All the light had now gone from the sky, and distantly we could hear Vespers being sung in deep men's voices, strange to our ears. Beside me Mother was murmuring the words to herself. Catherine and I were silent.

The door opened and we were invited in.

In the porch the almoner waited. He bid us welcome, but his voice was flat and dry, and I knew he had heard the story of our priory and that we were not welcome here.

"We have some accommodation for travellers," he said.

"Thank you."

"No doubt you will be moving on tomorrow." He led the way, lamp flickering, along a dark passageway and showed us to a room where a number of pallets were laid out.

"Please, " I said. "We need a fire for Mother. She is ill."

"Ill?" This was said sharply.

"Ill with a congestion in the chest. Nothing catching."

"I will send someone, and food and water. Goodnight Sisters."

A lay brother brought a brazier, and built up a fire in the hearth. I thanked him and he looked at me sideways and scuttled away, without speaking.

Soon, with the door closed, the room began to warm up. The food the brother brought was simple, bread and pease brose, no doubt the same as the Brothers themselves were having, and we were grateful for it.

We lay on the pallets, and stretched out our limbs in the warmth, and smelled the pinewood and peat of the fire, and fell asleep.

In daylight I could see the abbey was a fine one, larger than our priory, and built of a whiter stone. It lay protected in the hollow made by three hills, and a river ran along the southern edge. In summer, when the trees are clothed in green, it must be a beautiful place.

Our benefactors know that the worship of God is easier when the religious are surrounded by beauty. They choose the best places. No doubt that was why Lord Archibald wanted our priory, round which to build his fine new abbey.

For the first time since I left it, I allowed my mind to return in memory to Lincluden, tranquil in the curving arm of the Cluden Water, with the heron standing silently for hours, and the apple blossom in the orchard, and the meadow where our cow grazed. I would never see it again.

Mother became too ill to move and we had to stay.

The Abbot sent a priest, who gave her Viaticum, to prepare her for her final journey.

I watched him as he anointed her brow, her nose, her mouth, her ears and her breast with the holy oil.

The priest and I sat by her bedside through the long watch of the night. Catherine lay on her pallet, curled up, her back to us.

Once Mother woke, and I saw her fingers open and curl up. I reached out my hand and put it into hers. She sighed.

"I was walking beside St Ninian. He told me he has been caring for me on our journey. Was I asleep, Marjorie? Was it just a dream, d'you think?"

I stroked her hand, and thought how much I loved her, and thought how unjust it was that she, who had lived a harmless life, worshipping God, should become a wanderer and die in a place where she was not wanted. I thought of how I had become a thief, and of what had happened to Catherine.

She drifted into unconsciousness, and towards dawn, she died.

We buried her at noon, in a corner of the Abbey's graveyard, well away from the graves of the monks. The priest intoned the burial service. Only Catherine and I and the almoner were there, and the four lay brothers who lowered her body into the earth.

In all the time we were there I never saw the abbot.

"What will you do?" asked the priest.

"Travel to Whithorn, as we were doing," I said. "I hope we will find sanctuary there, and peace."

"Whithorn is a poor place, now that the pilgrims no longer come. The cathedral is falling into ruin. But I think there are some monks still there."

"One place is as good as any other," I replied.

Catherine and I packed up our clothes, such as they were. We were given food for the journey.

The priest was to walk with us part of the way, to show us the road. Half a morning's journey, and we breasted a hill, from where the priest pointed to the line on the horizon which was the sea.

"There," he said. "Keep going west. There are two large rivers, but there are settlements at the fords and the people will see you safe across. God be with you."

He turned and strode back to the abbey.

"Well Catherine," I said, for this was the first chance we had to talk together alone. "We are nearly at journey's end, if the priest is to be believed."

"I'm not going."

I looked at her.

"I'm going back. I belong to that man now. I'm going back there."

I seized her hands, as if to keep her with me by force. "Please Catherine, stay with me."

"I can't. There is no future for me in Whithorn, or anywhere else with good people. I will go back and serve him and have his children."

We embraced, and then she turned back towards the east.

When she was out of sight, I turned west, towards Whithorn.

I never saw her again.

Russian Tea

Mary Woodward

I remember the story. I think I remember the story. It flaps gently at the back of my mind like a little moth caught in a glass before it is released back into the night air. Maybe I remember enough to write it down, to release it into other people's minds. I play for time; I think maybe I should ring my aunt. She was there. It may have been more than sixty years ago but she has a good memory. She just might have the one or two details which will make it live. But then I pull back. No. She could say it wasn't like that. Not the way you heard. It was this. It was so. And what she says might not help. Might stamp it into oblivion.

I stay in all afternoon, do some filing, prepare a stack of blank paper. The story now and then gives itself a tremor, sends up a signal that it is still alive, that it can be rescued, lifted up. get away from here, possess itself.

Its visual reality deepens. At first it has the appearance of a stylish war movie. Great clothes. Wonderful setting. They've even got the hair perfectly right. My mother is twenty three, her dark waves are rolled up and kirbi-gripped in for the long and difficult journey back. She is standing on the platform at Kilfree Junction waiting for the noon Sligo to Dublin train. Her suit is very smart, navy blue wool, it cost her half a month's wages (she is a ward sister in Hackney Hospital in Oxford Street). She has hardly worn it during the last two weeks on holiday back home on their farm, only a couple of times for Mass and once when she visited the nuns at the convent for tea. Otherwise she has worn the cotton dresses and shorts and blouses now carefully packed in the suitcase at her feet.

She is trying hard not to cry as their father says goodbye to them. Her younger sister Nancy is starting to blink too fast and is talking too much. Their mother never comes to see them off, saying she has to keep an eye on the younger ones but they know it is because it is too painful. The train, hissing like a huge cat, slowly draws in along the platform with the sinister punctuality trains you don't want to catch always have. No one gets off. Along the platform there are five or six local people but they'll only be going as far as Boyle to the mart.

Their father hands them up their cases. 'Be good girls now,' he says as he always does at the last moment. It is his joke. They are meant to laugh. They manage wobbly smiles, knowing that really he still means it just as much as when they were five and seven. He stands faithfully there and waves as the train moves out and puts on a horrible speed away out of their own landscape.

They fall back into their seats and both of them cry. I wonder why they are going back, to a war, to bombs, to fire, to possible death. Even now, though my intellect knows the reasons – poverty, migration, work – I cannot understand how they could willingly have said goodbye on such a morning, and there was more than one, to their fields, their family, the peaceful cows, the green lanes, the hills, the clear streams, to return to the hell of London. But by Mullingar they have cheered up; Nancy has produced a flask of tea and two little triangles of soda bread and treacle and they are debating whether or not my mother should get engaged to Peter Cleary, who is working in Hammersmith for London Transport. Well before Dublin they have decided that she shouldn't. As the train arrives at Westland Row, Nancy pulls out an enamelled compact and a lipstick. She sweeps a little drift of Rachelle powder over her summer hay harvesting brownness, and shines up her mouth with a new coat of Holly Red to take on the capital. She becomes a very young Vivien Leigh in a patriotic movie about brave young nurses returning to their posts.

By now it is early evening. From here on they know things will start to go wrong. There is no other possibility. The boat could be late. Very late. The sea could be rough. It is not impossible the boat could be torpedoed. This marriage of war and nature guarantees crossings full of empty hours of waiting and anxiety. They are used to it. All around them in the bare waiting hall there are other girls travelling back to English employers, and young men in khaki returning to British regiments. The overcrowded air is full of talk and laughter but also the metallic undercurrent of anxiety. My mum is already longing to be back at home with her parents or safe in her room at the hospital, with her navy and white spotted dress ready for the morning, her starched linen cuffs waiting side by side on the dressing table.

Nancy puts her suitcase on its side and sits on it, very lightly, searching for a cigarette at the same time. There is enough smoke in the air to make the other side of the hall half lost in greyness in the low wattage lighting. She is as smartly dressed as my mother in a black suit with a yellow and black striped silk blouse she bought in Jax at the Marble Arch end of Oxford Street. Though she works at a different hospital they meet on their days off to go shopping together. Always they buy things for their next holiday. This will be nice for Higgins' dance or for Mass, or Mammy'd like you in this. Then they have tea somewhere and go and see a film. Every week. Sometimes they have to go home with the shrapnel flying around during an air raid. But it doesn't put them off going out.

Eight o'clock, nine o'clock pass; boredom is giving way to real weariness. Then at last there is the ratcheting of bolts being pulled, doors opening, the heavy clankings from the quayside coming in with the cold air from the sea to the end of the Customs hall into which they now push. They take their turn to queue up at one of the trestle tables; their neatly packed things are expertly rolled around and glanced through by a sandy haired man who looks handsomer than he is in his braided cap. Nancy makes a joke about the diamond tiara under her jacket. He winks and then gives her case the same acclamatory chalk tick on the side as her sister's.

'Thank God,' she says as they inch their way on deck with the crowd, dive down the central staircase to the main lounge, on into the Ladies section at the far end, where they claim a length of battered maroon upholstery and spread out themselves and their bags. With luck they might hang on to enough room to be able to sleep. There are several girls their own age, some middle-aged women with elderly mothers. No babies, thank goodness.

They take turns to take a walk on deck; sailors finish hauling gantries; the engines begin to knock away dully somewhere in the hidden life of the hull. It is eleven and Dun Laoghaire is gone as Nancy takes a last look at the shore pulling away from them.

Back in the Ladies lounge the blue night lights are on, creating a shady

133

indigo quiet. They take off their shoes and stockings, put them tidily behind the suitcases so they will be able to find them quickly. Jackets over them, they fall asleep. It is a rough night. The ship reels like a heavy dancer; it hurls up and down but it knows the steps and they have done the crossing so many times they doze on, while all over the boat sick and nervous passengers cling to the rails, try to reach lavatories or decks before they start retching. Black foam spray hammers the deck and the windows of the lounges like a torrent of deliberately aimed marine venom. At five, still nowhere in sight of land, the weather eases a little. They are awake.

'Jesus, Kathleen, if I don't have a hot cup of tea I'll faint,' says Nancy. They find their shoes, decide to take their cases because it can't be that long before Holyhead surely, and make for the restaurant. There are a few others before them, survivors of the night before, who slept in here, heads down on the tables. At first it seems there is no other life, then a steward appears behind the counter with teapots and jugs, then another with a tray of bread rolls and little saucers of marmalade and margarine. A smell suddenly of hot fat from the galley behind seems to declare they have come through, no more chance of torpedoes, no more bad weather, no more sickening, lurching night.

With their big cups of tea and two little packets of Marie biscuit they sit over by the windows to watch for the Welsh coast. The restaurant fills up around them. At the table next to them, sitting behind my mother but facing Nancy, there is a man in Royal Navy uniform, a lieutenant's dark suit, cap on the table. He too is drinking tea, and smoking, and scanning the oil-grey horizon.

Nancy kicks my mother neatly under the table and gestures with her eyebrows, only a millimetre but her sister doesn't miss it, to look over her shoulder. She does so. He is, of course, extremely handsome: dark brown hair, very blue eyes, an understructure of intelligence in his good looks. However, my mother, while supposedly nearly engaged to Peter Cleary has her mind on an English soldier she met some weeks before in London. So her glance at the sailor is neutral. Nancy is undeterred. She catches his eye.

'Terrible weather.'

'Terrible. but not as bad as at home.'

'Where are you from?'

'Galway. Just outside.'

'We're from the West too. Sligo.'

'The Wild West.' They all smile at this oh so familiar little joke.

'And where are you two off to?'

'London. We're nurses. Well, I'm a nurse and Kathleen here's a sister,' says Nancy. This pleases my mother who is notoriously proud of what she's achieved. 'And what about you?' Nancy knows he is more than likely to be going to Liverpool, will get off the boat train at Crewe.

'I don't know,' he says but what he means, of course, is I can't tell you.

'We're nursing with girls from Galway. Do you know an Ellen McShane?'

'No.'

'Gracie Tivnan?'

'No'

'Bridget Tansey?'

'No. No. Wait. Bridie Tansey. Not Bridie Tansey? With red hair?'

'She's the staff nurse on Kathleen's ward,' says Nancy with enormous satisfaction that she has been able to produce someone he does know, when there he was so smugly saying no as if it were impossible they could know anyone in common.

And of course at this point he comes and sits at their table. They buy more tea and share out cigarettes. It turns out that his brother was engaged to Bridie Tansey but it finished badly. Holyhead is sighted. He stays with them in the melee to disembark. Customs is faster here in the cold air of dawn and Nancy doesn't crack her joke about the diamond tiara a second time.

James Maguire, as my mother told me he was called, helps them find seats on the waiting train and they sit together as if they've been friends from childhood. He puts their cases up on the rack and then they all settle to watching the waves shoving up at the train as it steams along the embankment out of Anglesey to the mainland.

'You must know where you're off to next,' says Nancy, by now wild with curiosity about him.

'Arrah, Nancy, quit. He can't tell you.'

'I can, I suppose. Part of it. I'm on the Russian convoys.'

'Jesus, that must be cold.'

'Cold's only the half of it.' They have heard, or read rather, about these convoys. In the East End Churchill's about-turn to support the Russians has gone down well. It is welcomed, a relief to have an ally who seems to be determined to fight.

'What ship are you on?'

'Well now, I can't tell you that.'

'What kind of a ship then? A destroyer?'

'Or that.'

Whatever he was going to join, battleship, destroyer, cruiser, sloop, corvette, he was not saying; but they knew without him telling them what the sea must be like: the Irish sea multiplied ten times over, incandescent with storm and ice even in the summer, darkness all round the clock in the winter months, unending light and nowhere to hide from the Luftwaffe twenty four hours a day in summer.

'Have you stopped in Russia?'

'Once. In Archangel.'

'What was it like?'

'Grim. Air raids all the time. Grand if you like vodka.'

'Do you?'

'No.'

Nancy unclips her handbag. She is so proud of it, a black calfskin clutch with a silver clasp that she'd saved up weeks and weeks for when she first saw it in Dickins and Jones. She would play with its fastening just to draw attention to it but this time she rummages around inside and from the scented tombola of gloves, handkerchiefs, lipstick, powder compact and tube of Silvermints she pulls out a two ounce bar of Cadbury's chocolate. She snaps apart the squares and puts a small pile in front of each of them.

'There now. Elevenses.'

'We can buy tea at Crewe.'

'Aren't you getting off there?

'No.' He gives in. 'No. Yes. I'm going to London. After that 'tis a mystery. To me as much as you.'

The talk returns to Bridie Tansey and why she and his brother, John, had broken up.

'My parents weren't too keen. And she sensed it.'

'Why not? Didn't they like her?'

'Oh, they liked her well enough.'

'Are you farmers?'

'No. My father's a doctor. And so was my mother before she married him. She's English.'

Oh. They can see now only too well why Bridie, pretty and bright but one of twelve from a tiny smallholding half way up a mountain, had not been suitable. But then, it wasn't his fault, not this James Maguire. Surely he wasn't like that himself? But for the first time the conversation between them stalls. He is a little uncomfortable.

'Is Bridie courting now?'

'She is,' said Nancy with some satisfaction that she could speak of their friend and colleague as a girl who had not been destroyed by being cast off by the Anglo-Irish middle classes. 'In fact she's engaged. To an English pilot.'

There is a silence which says - so much for that John Maguire and well done Bridie Tansey. James has the grace to smile in acknowledgement of this.

'I'd better not tell John, He'd be very cut up. He hasn't met anyone else.'

And serve him right, the girls think as would any woman hearing the story. He sees a change of topic would be discreet.

'You're a brave pair of girls staying in London.'

'We've no choice.'

'You have. You could work somewhere else. You could go to America or back home.'

'We'd be bored back at home. There's nothing to do.'

'You're not frightened in the raids?'

'Sometimes.'

'I'd be terrified.'

'But you're all right on your boat in the middle of nowhere?'

'Ah, but we can fire back.'

He buys them cups of tea from the platform stall, while the train waits at Crewe. The few seats left fill up and the entire carriage is packed with a mass of khaki. A few sailors struggle with white canvas duffel bags. They are proud to be seen with him with his nice face and his officer's uniform. Maybe it crosses my mother's mind for a moment that this might be Nancy's destiny to meet this sailor. But, no, the thought of his parents and Bridie Tansey wipes out the possibility before it takes real shape. They are as poor as the Tanseys, No chance of anything, But maybe Nancy is too young to see this, maybe for an hour or two on that train heading for London she did think Is this him?

Outside Rugby, somewhere, in the middle of the tidily ploughed Midland fields the train stops. You just never knew. Five minutes. An hour. Five hours. No point in even trying to guess. Once, at night, travelling to Holyhead, the train had stopped and not moved for seven hours. There was a huge raid nearby, Coventry or Birmingham, screaming on in the distance, across the sky, like an apocalyptic thunderstorm, infinitely malevolent while they stay jammed together in the dark carriages, trying to sleep and longing for the hiss of steam getting up in the locomotive. Today at least, thank God, it is daylight and it can't be a raid delaying them. The two girls fall asleep, and James Maguire reads the News Chronicle he's bought at Crewe. When they wake up he is doing the crossword. They help him with the clues for the rest of the journey.

'Will you be going to Archangel this time?' says Nancy as the train at last slips through Watford and everyone starts to stretch and find coats, and gather their things together. She says it with no more emphasis than if he'd possibly be staying in Brighton.

'Well, I might. Can I bring you anything back?' he says, equally easily as if he were going to be asked to bring back a stick of rock.'

'What do they have in Archangel, Kathleen, for God's sake?'

My mother thinks hard. It is a chance to give him an address, for them to stay in touch with him. What can they ask for? From Russia? All she knows about Russia is that they eat caviar. No use asking for that. Or vodka. No one back home in Sligo would give you a thank you for either. And no point in asking for sweets or stockings or perfume. Then she remembers their mother grumbling about how expensive the tea had become in Stensons. They might not have rationing in the Republic, but the wartime market has its own equally powerful ways of limiting supplies.

'Tea. You could send our mother some tea. Do you have tea on those convoys?'

James Maguire thinks of the decks of the merchant vessels chained full with fighter planes and tanks and jeeps, and the holds stuffed with ammunition and guns and barrelfuls of fuel. But there was the odd small, slow, stocky ship carrying Empire foodstuffs the Russians asked for too, Spices, coffee, and yes, tea. Some tea.

'We might. Give me your mother's address.' He pushes the News Chronicle towards them with the pencil he's been using to fill in the crossword. Nancy writes across the top Mrs Scanlon, Clooneigh. Near Ballymote, Co Sligo.

'I can't promise but I'll try.'

But as he leaves them when they turn off for the tube at Euston he suddenly sees clearly how young they are, and how far from home, and how vulnerable. And as he goes for the taxi rank, he shouts across to them and laughs, 'I'll do my best about that tea. I will now.'

Months went by, black months of fatigue and destruction. For a while James Maguire steps out of the human reality of this story which takes such an act of will to resurrect; he fades into the distant cold of the Arctic seas. Research cannot tell which ship he was on – HMS Achates, or Palomares or the Lark, the Hardy, the Trinidad, the Matabele, the Bramble, the Bluebell, or any one of all the others, cruiser or battleship or corvette. He could be on one of many Flower class corvettes, really just redesigned whalers with guns, and for some reason all of them named after English flowers: HMS Snowdrop, HMS Campanula, HMS Spiraea, HMS Oxlip, and on and on, a whole vast armed garden of them. Can anything more unlikely be taking on U boats, with only their sinister numbers to mark them?

Other facts are easy to discover. All the figures are there on the cargoes needed to equip an army on the Eastern front: the nearly 8 million rounds of .5" Vickers ammunition, and the guns to go with it, the 30,727 miles of telephone cable, the 40,000 tons of raw copper, the thousands

139

and thousands of fighter aircraft and tanks, the 15 million pairs of boots, all that and much more stashed into or lashed onto those desperately slow merchant ships crewed by men who had never meant to sign up for anything like this; the bewildered Chinese and Arab sailors who found themselves in the Arctic storms with the Luftwaffe bearing down at them and the submarines steadfast in the depths beneath them. Somewhere with them, trying his best to fight the unbelievable cold and the lack of sleep and the ever present threat of attack, in a woollen duffel coat and thick long johns is James Maguire.

The girls return to their jobs and forget about him. They have met hundreds of young men risking their lives one way or another. They don't take any of them very seriously. The holiday before they had met two handsome Americans on the boat to Ireland, who had asked them where they were staying in Dublin so they could collect them for a night out. The Gresham, Nancy had said, knowing that by the evening they would be alighting at Kilfree and, anyway, never in their whole lives would they be able to afford to stay at the Gresham. So James Maguire does not linger in their memories for very long.

Now and then there is an occasional reference to the Russian convoys in the press, reminders that somewhere the Anglo Russian alliance is expressing itself in real terms: allied bullets hit grey uniforms, American jeeps hurtle down Soviet roads, Indian spices in Colonial style tins enliven Red Army kitchen supplies.

What is to be hoped is that he was not with the doomed convoy PQ 17, that he was not on one of its escorts, HMS Fury or Ledbury maybe, or the corvettes Dianella or Poppy, because that would have broken his heart for ever, to have to live with the memory of the merchant ships they deserted, ordered to flee by a high Command unnerved by the possible nearness of the mighty battleship Tirpitz. He'd never forget the overladen lumbering ships, many of them American, left to the enemies waiting in the sky and sea, an abandonment which soured relations between the Royal Navy and the Merchant Marine, and the United States Navy, for years, caused many a fight in harbour pubs, was still causing libel suits in the 1960's.

*Sorry to leave you like this. Goodbye and good luck. It looks a
bloody business.*

Signal from Commander Jack Broome,
Senior officer of the PQ17 escort.

James Maguire becomes a player in the saddest of sea tragedies with,
incredibly, Douglas Fairbanks Jr. there as an officer on the USS Wichita,
as if what happens has not enough power already to catch our
imaginations. If James was on one of PQ 17's treacherous escorts, was
actually on the Dianella, he survived its reeling decks, the constant
watches, the diet of flabby corned beef, to reach Archangel, where he
stayed for a cold and dull three months trying to like vodka, and making the
most of the occasional football match with the local sailors. We know he
survived, unlike the seamen found by the Russian ship the Murmantz, a
sad wreckage of bobbing orange life-jackets among the floating sacks of
flour, unlike all the others never found, never even looked for.

Nancy and my mother had two weeks holiday the following winter. The
crossing was fine, the delays not as bad as they might have been. Their
father, in his best suit of course, met them at Kilfree and carried their cases
back across the fields. The younger children ran down to meet them. The
Christmas supplies had been bought: jam, a sack of sugar and a tin of
biscuits. And at night there was no black-out, not that the soft light of their
oil lamp could have been seen too far off.

They have brought a few presents, some hankies they've embroidered
with initials, and some comics, and a lipstick for their mother. They hide
these in their cases and put them on the top of the wardrobe in their
parents' room where the little ones are not allowed to go. There is nothing
so wonderful as the first night home and though they could go to a dance
somewhere towards Boyle they stay in. Their mother puts on a kettle over
the turf smouldering in the hearth. She goes to the dresser for the teapot
and cups and saucers. While she is there she says something over her
shoulder to them. They do not quite catch it.

'What?'

141

'And the tea you sent has been grand.'

'What?'

'The tea you sent.'

'We haven't sent you any tea. We can't get tea.' Their mother points to the back of the dresser. There is a large wooden box behind the jug and the china.

'It arrived last week. I thought you must have sent it through a friend. I didn't know the writing.'

'Where was it posted from?'

'Arragh, how would I know that?'

'The stamps'.

'It had British stamps on. But the box has funny letters on it. Foreign looking.'

'Foreign looking how?'

She brings the teapot over to the fire and fills it with boiling water. She is a little exasperated by all this.

'It doesn't make sense to me.'

'Wasn't there a note or anything?'

'No'.

By now Nancy is holding the box. The Cyrillic does not make sense to her either. This is not so much a box as a small crate. She slides aside the opening slat on the top. Inside it is lined with heavy metallic paper and is almost full of black tea. She sniffs it. The dry leafy fragrance is subtle and even. This is expensive tea. Fine tea. Tea which would grace porcelain with gilded rims, with sky blue cherubs painted among green and silvery foliage, clinking lightly next to silver spoons in rose-scented drawing rooms. Tea for another world.

'It's the best tea I've tasted, wherever it comes from,' says their father.

For a moment they, and we, can see James Maguire on the quayside in Archangel. He is talking to one of the sailors on a merchant ship from PQ17, one of the few which did manage to come through, maybe the Empire Tide. They were together in the football team last weekend and have met by chance a few times in one of the dark and festeringly busy little bars which try to serve the whole of Archangel. The sailor is from Calcutta and has worked on the Empire Tide for the past five years. But those were the calm old journeys bringing spices and striped Indian silks to Liverpool He whistles through his teeth with horror when he talks about the catastrophic voyage they have only just survived. Never again, he says, never bloody again. I'm going to stop in Liverpool and get a job on the ferries.

Last night James asked him what the Empire Tide was unloading. Cooking oils and spice. And coffee and tea. For the politicians, he says, shaking his head. James promises him a good price for a small box of this tea. He meets him early in the morning when the quayside is busy but there are not enough Soviet inspectors around to query the transaction. James hands over a couple of notes. With luck he will be leaving port in the next couple of days.

The tea goes into the bottom of his duffel bag wrapped in a towel. The journey is not without its panics and alarms but the Dianella makes her way, unholed, to Reykjavik and then back to Glasgow. At this point James thinks of writing a note to go in with the box but he is in a hurry. He has two days' leave and he wants to get to Edinburgh to meet up with some old friends from school. And besides, when it comes to it he cannot think of anything to say. Maybe he is too depressed by what he has been part of to want to write to anyone at the moment. Or maybe the girls on the Holyhead boat train are fading from his memory too. All he has is the recollection that he made this promise lightly yet it is a challenge to live up to it. Maybe keeping his word on this will start to redeem for him what has happened to PQ 17, for that moment when, disbelieving, he stood on deck and felt the Dianella change course 20' east and move away, upping her knots like an untrustworthy collie which has turned away from its sheep and fled for home. For the rest of his life, perhaps, he has become the sort of man who never fails to do what he said he'd do as if he can, by that, expiate the fate of the twenty five doomed ships they were supposed to protect.

He has kept the address folded up in his wallet. The box is wrapped in brown paper from Woolworths and a piece of string he finds in the wardroom. He finds time to rush into a small post-office on his way to catch the bus, and then the tea is safe, on its way to the Republic.

It lasts a good few months, even though tea drinking is a day long, night long pursuit in Clooneigh. When my mother and Nancy go back to London in the New Year of 1943 they take some in a large brown envelope and divide it up between when they arrive. It makes fine cups of tea in the cold, early spring evenings and mornings. After that they are at the mercy of rationing for the foreseeable future. They never hear of James Maguire again.

And even as I write he vanishes for a second time, even more completely. Researching this story I check his name on the Internet. 'James Maguire, Russian Convoys,' and yes, there is a result. But it isn't a man. There is a James Maguire, wonderfully enough, but it is a merchant ship, not a human being. Is that what my mother said? He was on a ship called the James Maguire. Did she misremember? Have I got it wrong? Did I only half-listen to her on one of those Sunday afternoons when I'd read the papers and occasionally she would tell me some little memory or another? She's dead now so I can't check. In the end, after I have written most of this, my Aunt Nancy rings me for a chat. I ask her about James Maguire but she can't remember him. She remembers the Americans she misled about the Gresham. But James Maguire? Nothing.

But I know this happened. I know what my mother told me. There was a sailor. And there was the box of tea, and it did make its way from the Arctic Circle to the farm in Country Sligo. And in trying to rebuild this little story I have hit, as if it were an iceberg itself, the vast truth, the huge, terrible, undoubtedly real story of PQ 17 and the deserted merchant ships trying desperately to keep up with their trusted Royal Navy escorts, even as they sped away from them; and the circling predatory U-boats and planes; and the dozens and dozens and dozens of merchant seamen lost in a sea so cold that even the best swimmer had no chance of survival; and, as in all wars, the disastrous orders issued from too far away, in panic or misunderstanding or callousness, and the commanders who dispense death as if human lives were no more than tea leaves in a cup.

Winner of the Short Histories Prize — Jo Campbell

began writing after a career as a civil servant. Her work has appeared in a number of anthologies: most recently she came second in the *Fish Short Story Prize* for 2005. *All the King's Horses* is her first attempt at historical fiction, a challenge she found immensely stimulating. Jo is married with two grown-up children and lives in London. Apart from writing, her interests include theatre, travel, and incessant reading

Second in the Short Histories Prize — Hugo Kelly

has been writing for a number of years and at this stage should really know better. A master of shortlists he has been twice nominated for a *Hennessy Award*, and the *Fish Short Story Prize* amongst others. His work has appeared in the *Sunday Tribune*, the 1998 and 2004 *Fish Anthology*, the *Cúirt Annual*, *Books Ireland* etc. During peaceful breaks from his Librarian job in Galway, Hugo works on a much anticipated novel for children. Someday the stabilisers will come off the bike, but not just yet.

Third in the Short Histories Prize — Phil Jell

was born in Berkshire in 1978. After training at art school he moved to London to study at the Courtauld Institute, where he decided writing fiction was more interesting than researching for a Masters degree. He has worked as a photographer, TV scene painter, gardener and just about everything else to keep himself in ink and paper. He currently works part time for the Imperial War Museum whilst putting the finishing touches to his first novel. 'Altarpiece' is his first work of historical fiction. Phil lives in Nunhead, South London.

Emma Darwin

was brought up in London, Manhattan and Brussels. Distractions have included academic publishing, two children and a darkroom, but her novel *The Mathematics of Love* is due out from Headline Review in July 2006 and in the USA in 2007. Her story *Maura's Arm* was placed at Bridport 2004. Emma's a glutton for punishment: she's following her MPhil in Writing from Glamorgan with a PhD at Goldsmiths'. Just as exciting but much nearer home, if asked, she'll admit to being a great-great-granddaughter of Charles Darwin.

Judy Crozier

Judy Crozier's first book, when she was eleven, was filled with characters whose names were Judy's friends', only backwards. This is very effective, and highly recommended for that touch of mysterious foreignness. Until that time, Judy and her family were in Vietnam where her father was an attaché with the Australian Embassy in the 1960s. This experience provided the background to Judy's first novel which is, incidentally, now in search of an agent. Judy lives in Melbourne, Australia, and her life has included election to a position in local government, community and political work, some journalism, and two grown-up children. Her writing is now receiving attention with significant awards for short stories, and some publication both at home and abroad. Currently she is undertaking a Masters degree in creative writing at Melbourne University.

Clare Girvan

has been a prize-winner in several short story competitions, including the *Ian St James* and the *Asham Literary Endowment Trust*, and is published in their anthologies. In 2000, the Asham story was chosen for a Radio 4 series of writing by women. She has written one novel, is halfway through her second, and researching for her third. Two of her plays have been performed at Exeter's Northcott Theatre, she recently directed *The Admirable Crichton* for Exeter's summer festival, and her adaptation of *Cold Comfort Farm* is to be staged in 2006. She is currently studying screenwriting, and makes and sells Fabergé-style eggs when she needs a holiday from brainwork. She lives in a pretty little coastal town near Exeter with her journalist husband and two cats, which all helps.

Sheila MacAvoy

was born in New York City, a descendant of Famine Irish peasants who hit the Big Apple in the 1850s; educated in local schools, eventually earning a Law Degree. Worked in Los Angeles, California, as a lawyer in the aerospace industry by day and wrote fiction by night. Published here and there, including appearance in the 1998 *Fish Short Story Prize* collection as a choice of the Editor. Exit aerospace. Some recent stories are forming a chrysalis which, if subjected to the right temperature and humidity, should morph into a Gold Rush saga, told through its many dreamers, past and present. View from work table is of the pink and white sandstone Santa Barbara Mission, a mile and a half distant, set against the chaparral of the Coast Range.

Imogen Robertson

was born in 1973 in Darlington, and now almost makes a living as a TV director in London. She is currently trying to wrestle her first novel, an eighteenth century murder mystery, to the floor.

Janette Walkinshaw

Janette Walkinshaw's many jobs have taken her to Paris, to the Clyde shipyards, a Highland estate, and self-sufficiency on a smallholding. She's had short stories published, and radio plays broadcast, and this has encouraged her to think there is a life beyond earning a living. She is presently writing on commission for BBC radio and continues to work on The Novel.

Mary Woodward

London Welsh/Irish – has an Irish passport though she was born in Hammersmith.

She has had poetry published in magazines such as *Poetry Ireland, the Shop, the North, Ambit, the London magazine* and one collection, about Berlin, – *Almost Like Talking* (Smith Doorstep 1993.)

Mary has taught literature, and, more recently, fashion. In 2004, she was the winner of the Guardian newspaper's *Jackie Moore Award* for Fashion Writing. In the same year she was a prize-winner in the *Arvon Poetry Competition.*

Mary has only recently started writing fiction seriously, and this is her first success. She is delighted that a story which means a lot to her personally was liked enough by the judges to be included in this anthology.

Authors Who Reached the Final Short List

in the Short Histories Prize

Lane Ashfeldt

Mary Bonner

Gerardine Burke

Jo Campbell

Stephan Clark

Judy Crozier

Emma Darwin

Carys Davies

Christina Davis

Waverley Fitzgerald

Solveig Foss

Clare Girvan

David Hart

Phil Jell

Hugo Kelly

Sheila MacAvoy

Fred McGavran

Anna Milford

Lucy Moore

Marc Phillips

Jean Pickering

Imogen Robertson

Richard Scott

Christine Stanton

Claire Thomas

Robin Tilley

Michele Torrey

Marja Ulpovaara-Greenlees

Janet Walkinshaw

Mary Woodward

About Fish Publishing

Fish is an independent outfit dedicated to fostering and publishing new talent. The Fish Short Story Prize has been running annually since 1994, and over 200 winning writers have been published in the resulting anthology. Many of these writers have subsequently developed successful careers.

Inspired by the success of the Short Story Prize, Fish Publishing, in partnership with the British Historical Novel Society, developed the Short Histories Prize. This book is testament to its success.

Fish also hosts an annual One Page Story Prize, and a Poetry Prize. The Unpublished Novel Award will be run again after the publication of the previous winner, Nick Wright's *The Language Me Feel It*.

Fish provides an extensive *Critique Service* which offers feed-back for writers' on a one-off basis and, for writers who require a longer-term assessment of their work, an *Editorial Consultancy Service*.

The Fish Short Story Prize is an open door that's inviting
writers to walk through it. It has to be encouraged,
celebrated, congratulated.
Roddy Doyle

Fish is doing great work. It's an inspiration for all new
writers.
Frank McCourt

DETAILS, ENTRY FEES AND ON-LINE ENTRIES FOR ALL
COMPETITIONS

and infor

CRITIQUE SERVICE AND

SE

See: **www.fis**

info@fishpublishing.c

Fish Publishing, Durrus,